THE MACH
STRATEGY

LANDO S. THOMPSON

outskirts
press

Outskirts Press, Inc.
http://www.outskirtspress.com

Paperback ISBN: 978-1-9772-1913-8

Library of Congress Control Number: 2019915305

Outskirts Press and the "OP" logo are trademarks belonging to Outskirts Press, Inc.

PRINTED IN THE UNITED STATES OF AMERICA

Thank you Brittney, for supporting me all the way through.

Never don a mask.

TURN 1.

Drafted

While I was sitting under the protective dome produced by the Blaze Luminous shield, I finally received the message. It read "You've been drafted! Welcome to the Hegemony's Military Forces." I tapped the Focus on the side of my head to move to the next page. "The Hegemony needs your support, Brandon Simons. You have been chosen to train in the Hegemony Sequence Academy of the Centauri Sector to be the Lieutenant of Platoon C. Pack your things because your Capsule group will leave date $\triangle$5 year 142 P.C.W. Your genetic pair will also be revealed to you date $\triangle$4 year 142 P.C.W. Welcome to the Hegemony's Military Forces!" I had two Cycles to pack my things before launch, and one Cycle until I meet the person who I'm supposed to mate with.

Dammit, Bradley, you just don't give us time to prepare!

I stood up from the bench I was sitting on and made my way to the nearest Teleport Point. The Blaze Luminous dome around the Xerxes Sector made everything have a slight green tint, making the skyline that much more unique. Of course Mars was fully terraformed and it wasn't needed, but the people living in Xerxes didn't want it to be taken down. In fact our Sector flag is designed to reflect the Blaze Luminous hexagonal pattern. A gentle breeze blew by, rustling the leaves around me. Fluffs of pollen floating among the breeze immediately incinerated on contact with the shield.

I made it to the Teleport Point and warped to my dorm. I sat down on my bed, bouncing a little, contemplating how much my life was about to change.

I'm going to be a Lieutenant... My one purpose is to serve the Hegemony. I should just stop thinking about this, it won't change anything.

The thought was somewhat painful, and lingered in my mind. I turned on the TV. to distract myself, and it buzzed to life. "The next Generation of Sequence Academy students will be launching in two delta Cycles. If the system is correct, these students will be genetically superior to the previous Generation in every way," read the news woman from her paper. She was old. I assumed she was part of Gen Gamma due to the fact that she was wearing reading glasses, a trait eliminated by genetic pairing two Generations ago. After about 30 minutes of speaking about the goal of Sequence Academy, she then went on with the usual propaganda: "Long live the Hegemon! Long live the Hegemony!" Then the broadcast ended.

My view of the Hegemony wasn't entirely bad. I acknowledge it as a good governing system. It was much better than having multiple governments with conflicting views. It also provided all people with food and housing for free. The only cost was required military service. The system was actually perfect in my mind.

I flopped back on my bed to stare up at the metallic ceiling. Power-rails pulsed through in small, nail-thin pathways to the single light that hung from it. I followed each individual pulse all the way to the light, watching them flow like a river driven by a heartbeat.

The silence in my dorm was finally broken by the sound of my dorm mate opening the door. "I see you're as pale as ever, my good friend!" he said. "You should explore the outside of the settlement!"

"Nice to see you too, Ryan." I could tell he had been outside because his blonde hair still had little fluffs of pollen stuck in it.

"Anyway," Ryan said as he sat down on his bed across from me, "did you see the message on your Focus?"

"Yeah," I responded.

"Cool! What were you drafted for?" he asked.

"I'm a Lieutenant. You?"

"I'm a Building Unit," he responded, grabbing the back of his neck.

"Oof! They basically put a target on your head," I joked.

"Haha, yeah. So what Platoon are you in, Lieutenant Brandon?" He gave a playful salute.

"I'm in Platoon C."

"Aww. I'm in B." His shoulders slumped.

"Well, I guess you won't have my military expertise."

"What expertise?"

"How dare you, sir!"

"Well, we should start packing for launch day."

"That's a smart idea." I stood and checked the window and noticed how late it was. While looking out into the skyline, I was mesmerized by Xerxes again. Seeing the pillar of light formed by the Typlar Gate and the Teleport Points always made me glad to be human. It was an intricate grid of buildings, all aligned to make a web of triangles seen from space. Hundreds of housing units were illuminated by the occupied rooms. I pulled out my bag and sat down. While I packed I thought that this might be my last few days seeing Ryan. Since he was in a different Platoon than me, he most likely would be in another housing unit. I would also be housed with my Pair. After a little bit I managed to trick myself into thinking that I would probably see him sometimes, just not as much as usual. We had spent five years in the same room together, just waiting for the day we would be sent off to the Sequence Academy. After a couple hours we had both finished packing everything we had and I started to feel as though I was ready to move to the Sequence Academy. At about 2100 I decided to go to bed.

TURN 2.

Paired
_____

My Focus woke me up at 0600. Ryan had already begun brushing his teeth and I was still disheveled from sleep. I sat up in bed and stared out into the Xerxes skyline for a minute before finally jumping out of bed. I went to the pantry to get some cereal then went to brush my teeth. By the time I finished, Ryan was out the door. I sluggishly made my way to the nearest Teleport Point to go to Central Gate. I walked across the sidewalk in the shade of the housing units. The sun was peeking over the horizon, mixing fading orange in the sky. I found a Teleport Point and let its light consume me to warp over to my destination.

Central was the busiest Sector of the Mars Colony. It had the largest population and was the place where Mars' Typlar Gate was built. Despite how frequently it was visited, there weren't many buildings. Central was mainly just a bunch of brick paths that led to the Typlar Gate, with a decent amount of vegetation strewn about. It clashed in a beautiful way with the massive industrial structures of Xerxes. This Typlar Gate was the most used gate in the Hegemony because it connected the Centauri System to the Birth System. Its streets were bustling with the conversations of thousands, all of them blending together into a melodic cacophony. When I made it to the gate I saw that the next Capsule would be arriving in 30 minutes.

While I waited, I was approached by a girl who appeared to be in my Gen Group.

"Hello," she said as she sat down in the seat beside me.

"Hello," I responded.

"Are you waiting for a Capsule too?" Her smile was warm and comforting.

"Yeah," I said.

"Man, this place is busy, isn't it?" she said, attempting to continue conversation.

"Well, it is Central..." I smiled slightly.

We both grew silent for a little bit until she continued.

"I'm Quinn Stokes, by the way." She reached out to shake my hand.

"Brandon Simons." When we shook hands, I got a good look at her. She was dark-skinned, with brown eyes. Her hair was in an afro and on her shirt it said *Sea of New Hope*.

"You're from the Capital?" I asked.

"Oh no, I'm from the Lotus Sector," she corrected me.

"Well, either way you're quite a ways from home," I joked.

"Oh yeah, good thing travel is free, right?"

"Yup."

We continued to talk for the remainder of the time until our Capsule came and we were seated in separate areas.

The Capsule was a gigantic cylinder divided into rotating circles that maintain simulated gravity. It descended from the sky and came to a stop on the platform. I boarded the Capsule and took my seat in Quadrant Four.

Before we launched for the Centauri System I noticed, outside the window, the world around the Capsule began to warp and get distorted. The outside world swirled itself into a nauseating pattern. This eventually stopped and the Capsule shot off into space, the initial launch rocked me around wildly in my seat. Watching the stars zip past was disorienting. After a couple of minutes the Captain got on the mic.

"Hello passengers, this is your Captain speaking. Our trip to the Alpha Centauri System is estimated to be complete in about two hours. That's right we are crossing 4.37 light years in two hours. This kind of technology is only developed by the Typlar Foundation, 'Bringing you Tomorrow Today.'"

The trip then went on normally. Snacks were provided to everyone, as well as Focus Network connection, but that was available everywhere. Pairs of roommates chatted quietly, awaiting our arrival.

Two hours finally passed and the Capsule landed, throwing me around even more than the launch. The Captain cut onto the audio again and said "Thank you for traveling with us this fine Cycle. Your Focus should automatically help you adjust to the difference in gravity. If help is needed, please head to Quadrant Four, Division A."

When I stood up my body felt heavier than usual, making it a little strange to walk. With two taps of my Focus, my head tingled and my body adjusted, still leaving me a little uneasy, but better nonetheless. I exited the Capsule and found myself in a place busier than Central.

Amestris had the largest population in the Hegemony. It was a beautiful landscape to behold. Housing Buildings cut the sky apart, reflecting the sunlight back down to the people walking to their destinations. The monument to the Viceroy stood tall in the center of the plaza. The plate on its base read *Viceroy Micah, Leader of Amestris*. Pod ships flew between the mazes of buildings that were Amestris, in swarms. A Holo-rail was just making its way past when I spotted Ryan. For some reason I did not approach him. I continued to walk as though I hadn't seen him. I and many others were heading to the Generation Center. This was a massive dome for scientific research and the meeting place of the Genetic Pairs.

The room was dark, with the main light coming from the spotlight that shone on the red curtain of the stage and the light emitted from our Focuses. I sat down in a random seat and waited for the speaker to get on stage. After five minutes a tall, slender man suddenly warped onto the stage.

"Greetings Generations Zeta and Epsilon, I am Dr. William Vallor, developer of the Vallor Focus Network, and also representative of this Gen Group." His eyes were droopy, and sad. His black hair was thinning, leaving him with a noticeable widow's peak. He had a mild country accent which was the only source of energy for his speech. "This Cycle," his voice droned on, "you all will be meeting your Genetic Pair. This person has been matched with you for the sole purpose of advancing the human race by producing an offspring that is genetically superior to the Gen Group before it. I would now like to ask you to activate your Focuses and join hands with the person who is highlighted." I tapped my Focus and I was directed to my left.

The girl I saw was thin but clearly a good runner, a good trait for a Unit. She had red hair, green eyes and a Hegemon Loyalty tattoo on her neck. She turned and was somewhat surprised at how close I was. We both walked towards each other and joined hands. I checked my Focus to learn her name.

"So you're Brandon Simons?" she asked me.

"Yup, and you're Nina Glass?"

"Yup." She smiled at me.

Now that we were closer together, I could tell she was just a little shorter than me and she had a mild British accent. She was wearing a grey hoodie that read Amestris.

"You're from here?" I asked

"Yeah, where are you from?"

"Xerxes" I said.

"Ooo, I hear it's a pretty Sector, but it's kinda far from here."

"Yeah, I had to take a Capsule."

"Oh God, I hate those things."

"Really?"

"Yeah, I hate sitting still for that long, and I can't even look out the window without getting sick."

"Do you mind if I ask you what Unit class you are?"

"I'm a Thief Unit in Platoon C."

"Well I guess I'm your Lieutenant."

She chuckled "Well that's a coincidence, isn't it?"

Right before I could respond Dr. Vallor began speaking again. "Hopefully you all have found your Genetic Pairs. Okay? Good. Now, before I let you all get to know each other and find your fellow Platoon mates, I will need to tell you this one law. Any offspring produced by those who are not Genetic Pairs, will be terminated. Y'all got that?" There was a unanimous sound of acknowledgement. "Good, now be free!"

"Hey, I'm going to go find the Squad leaders." I told Nina.

"I'll join you." she replied.

I used my Focus to scan the surrounding people. Conveniently all my squad leaders were grouped together. Nina and I approached them.

"Hello," I said. "I am Brandon Simons, Lieutenant of Platoon C."

TURN 3.

Ranks

I extended my hand to give one of the five people in front of me a handshake. Without warning I suddenly had an arm around me.

"Nice to meetcha, Brandon! My name is Eric Hensley." Eric shoved a translucent card into my hand that had his name and strengths chart on it. He spoke with the same eccentricity of a news caster from the old world.

"So you're my Shield leader then." I said, still bewildered by his enthusiasm. Eric was substantially taller than me and had a much sturdier build. He wore a Hegemon Pride tattoo on his forehead. He was also unnaturally pale, so I assumed he was from the Xing Sector, the moon.

"Um," I heard a quiet voice say. "I'm Dayami Parker." I uploaded Eric's data to my Focus and took her strengths chart. The card said *Sniper*. "I'm Eric's Genetic Pair," she spoke again. "You're not the only one getting used to his... energy." She was about the same height as Nina. Her stance was timid and her eyes were shy, keeping her distance slightly behind Eric.

"Well I'm sorry," Eric joined in, and took his arm from over my shoulder.

"It's nice to see a Sniper in my Platoon," I said in response to seeing the card.

THE MASK OF STRATEGY

"Oh yeah, it is kinda rare to be chosen as one."

I then was assaulted by a short girl with black hair and an Asian complexion. "If this was a real mission you'd be dead by now," she said while holding me in a choke hold with her left hand on the side of my head.

"Well done, you've killed a Lieutenant," I responded.

"Emery Forbes" She shook my hand. "I didn't really feel like bringing my card because you'll see me next Cycle."

"Well, you should at least tell me what Unit you are."

"I'm a Thief."

"Oh! I'm a thief too!" Nina blurted.

"Glad to have you aboard," Emery said.

Nina extended her hand to make the interaction more formal but Emery refused. "That would be a bit difficult."

"Why?"

Emery then showed everyone her hands. In her palms were Thief plates. "They create the AOE around my hands to form the conversion barrier." The plates were large circles that covered Emery's palm. In the center of each shone a smaller circle, containing a substance that I only knew the name of, orichalcum.

"Oh shit... I just remembered I need to get them attached at Sequence Academy."

"Don't worry," Emery said, "it only hurts for a couple hours."

I was then approached by a slender average height man with a Hegemon purity tattoo on his arm.

"Lieutenant Brandon, I am Giovanni Sosa, leader of the Blade squadron." He then handed me his card. "And unlike *some* people, I was not too lazy to bring my card to a formal event." His blue eyes darted over at Emery.

"Aw shut up," she said.

I looked at his card. His stats were seemingly flawless. Before I could address this I was cut off by Dr. Vallor. "It is now 1000. May I please have all Sequence Academy attendees exit the building, and have all Majors and Generals meet in the conference room."

"Well I guess we should go now." Eric said "I'll see you all at training."

"I might as well get going too. See ya' later kid." Nina poked me with her elbow.

"Aren't I older than you?"

"Don't know, don't care," she said while walking off towards the south exit.

TURN 4.

Launch

I got off the Capsule at Xerxes around 1236. After Amestris, Xerxes seemed the quietest place in existence. I sat slumped in my dorm, exhausted, not even fully aware of what was happening on the news. All I heard was something about how the new Sequence Academy students were the future and how we would better the human race and other random stuff. Ryan came in at around 1322. "Where have *you* been?" I asked jokingly.

"I was out with my Pair," Ryan responded

"And who would that be?"

"Her name's Quinn."

"Stokes?"

"Yeah, you know her?"

"We met at the gate."

"Did you think she was from the capital too?"

"Yeah"

"Well anyway, who's your Pair?" Ryan asked eagerly.

"Her name's Nina." I told him.

"Okay, was she cute?"

"Yes? I'd say she's a little above average."

"Oof! I should tell her you said that."

"No!"

We continued with our usual routine for the Cycle until our Focuses told us to sleep early for the upcoming launch. Through the night I could hear the Capsule being tested before △5.

My Focus woke me up a little bit later than Ryan. I somewhat hurried to get ready but Ryan waited for me so I had rushed for no reason. We both warped over to Central to catch the Capsule which had already arrived and was boarding. I saw a particularly short boy get bombarded by newsagents and become overwhelmed. Before I got on the Capsule I got a message from Nina on my Focus.

Hey kid, I'm waiting in quad 3 seat 137.

"Who was that?" Ryan asked.

"Nina. She wants me to sit with her."

"Aww," he teased.

"Shut up."

I waved goodbye to Ryan and made my way up the Capsule to Nina and sat down.

"Oh, wow, you listened!" she said sarcastically and patted the seat for me to sit down.

"I thought you hated these things."

"I do, I just have no choice but to ride it."

I noticed how she was fidgeting with her hands and tapping her foot restlessly. I took a piece of gum from the tray table next to me and waited for launch. A few minutes later, Emery and Giovanni sat down across from us. "Hello Lieutenant." Giovanni said as he sat down.

"You don't need to call me Lieutenant yet, you know that right?" I responded

"*He won't stop.*" Emery messaged me. I noticed she was also tapping her foot restlessly like Nina. It must have been Unit conditioning.

Two minutes before launch, Eric and Dayami sat down next to me. Eric was strangely silent but I didn't question it. The Captain cut onto the mic and essentially said the same thing as last time but the only difference was that the flight was three hours instead of two. "Lord in heaven, not *another* hour on this thing," Nina groaned.

"Ugh, I hate riding these too." Emery said propping her head up with her hand.

"And I have the Plate surgery too after this."

"Well I don't know about you guys, but I'm going to sleep so try to stay quiet." Eric interrupted.

I sat back in my seat and put on some footage of the high level Skirmishes at the Sequence Academy to study their tactics. This went on for about an hour until I saw another message from Emery that she had apparently sent to everyone except Giovanni who was asleep in his chair. It said *"Watch this."* When everyone looked at her she pointed to Giovanni and tapped her Focus. He screamed and yanked off his.

"You vile woman," he screamed. "How dare you wake me with the sounds of your vulgar music!" He threw his Focus at her. Emery continued to laugh hysterically for the next minute or two before disconnecting the sound and handing Giovanni his Focus. After that the flight was somewhat boring. We eventually arrived at Sequence Academy around 1535. On the mic, someone other than the Captain began speaking.

"Welcome Generation Groups Zeta and Epsilon. I am Colonel Roy Mendez. I am leader of the Strategic Combat classes for Lieutenants here at The Sequence Academy. If you look out your windows, you will see Proxima B, which means that leaving the Sequence Academy without a ship or gate access is impossible. Gate access can only be given by the Generals, and I highly doubt they would give you children that power. Before you exit, activate your Focus Network reactor to check yourself off for attendance."

I exited the Capsule with the others and beheld the elaborate design of the Sequence Academy. There was a large Blaze Luminous dome around the entire station, which was a giant ring with the Typlar gate in the middle. On the ring were multiple rotating segments to generate artificial gravity just like in the Capsules. There was also an area that branched off from the main station. It was a gigantic black sphere, nothing else around it.

We walked towards a single doorway with the first step into the hall I couldn't hold myself to the ground. I drifted upwards, which forced me to grab onto a ledge in the wall to shoot myself forwards. Once on the other side of the doorway, I crashed to the floor, and watched as everyone else in my Platoon landed gracefully.

Inside the station, there were multiple different colored light paths that led to different areas. I noticed many people following those paths with jumpsuits that matched the colors.

Colonel Mendez warped in front of our group of amazed teenagers and directed us toward two massive auditoriums. One had a sign that read UNITS. The other read LIEUTENANTS. I said goodbye to my team and entered the Lieutenants auditorium.

On the massive metallic stage stood a strongly built, tall bald man with a black bushy mustache. His expression was stern, but his nose was distractingly large.

"Good afternoon, Launchies," his voice boomed. "I am General Felix Garner of the Z.E. Division however, you may call me Sir!" As he spoke, his mustache wiggled on his face, covering his lips. "When you are speaking to me, you will begin every sentence with Sir, and you will end it with Sir. Now, I would like to personally welcome you all to Sequence Academy. If the system is correct, you all should be genetically superior to me and all other students attending. Because you are all Lieutenants, you will have this week to move into your housing units, learn the layout of the building and get used to your classes.

TURN 5.

Sequence

General Garner appeared to have captured the attention of everyone in the room. Everyone who was holding a conversation in secret had gone silent, waiting for the explanation of the iconic ritual of The Sequence Academy: *Sequence*. The reasoning behind the name is still unknown and probably will never be revealed, because the creator of this game, the First Hegemon, is dead and did not disclose the reasoning behind the name all the way to his death.

General Garner continued: "Sequence will help you develop your naturally strategic minds. Of course the only guidance I will be able to give you are the rules of this game." There followed a dramatic pause. Next to him, a vortex of neon red sparks of light formed. From the spiraling madness emerged the shape of a person. This person's right arm had what appeared to be a laser projector. "This is a Blade Unit," Garner told us. "Your main assault piece, it is also one of your most versatile pieces." Garner said while pointing at the motionless student. The student, on command drew his weapon. His hand went into a karate chop position, and around it formed a neon red Blade extension. "This and many other Unit specific weapons have two modes: Training and Battle. Training mode is for Platoon skirmish simulations. Battle mode is for Academy matches. In both modes, each Unit has a Nano-Reactor. This Reactor, when it takes substantial damage, will cause your Unit to be destroyed. Allow me to demonstrate."

Garner put his hand into the same position as the defenseless soldier. His Blade was a neon, shimmering, brilliant green. Garner slashed the soldier into two halves, which almost instantly dissipated into the cloud of neon red sparks that the soldier had started off as. "Since he was wearing his Nano-Reactor" Garner said, "this soldier can be revived, meaning that another soldier on his team could run through this cloud and return him to an advancing state. The state you see now is the downed state." Another soldier appeared on the stage the same way the first did. They ran through the cloud, and it spiraled into the shape of a Blade Soldier. "The goal of this game is to eliminate all opposing forces so the enemy cannot revive."

Garner continued: "The next important part of this game is the Builder Unit. This Unit creates the terrain essentially. The Builder creates neutral nodes. These nodes can be activated by any side, though once activated by one team, it will say on that team's laser color until stolen by a Thief. These nodes once activated turn into lasers that are similar to the Blade's sword, but much more like a Blaze Luminous. This large laser wall will move or rotate however the builder wants it to. If you are in possession of a node it will become your color, and will move according to the code put into it by the Builder. If the enemy runs into this wall, he or she will be put into their downed state. This Unit was put in place to help students account for the unpredictability of war."

He paused again to let everyone take in the information he was throwing at us. "In the chance of aerial attacks in war, you will go to the Fleet Bay. Using a ship takes away the Unit class system in exchange for pulse blasts from the ship."

"This concludes my introduction. I would like to again welcome you all to Sequence Academy, and hopefully you will all adjust well." General Garner warped away.

The mess hall was like any school cafeteria. Multiple rows of tables surrounded by chattering students enjoying the food provided to them. I didn't see any one I recognized so I sat at one of the empty tables with my food. I decided that I would use this time to develop the skeleton of any strategies I would use in battle, some of which I was sure had already been tried before, though some I thought were entirely original. On the gigantic Holo-Projector on the west wall were the standings of the last two matches of the Cycle. Ada Stephens, Gen Epsilon Lieutenant of Platoon ◇ (Diamond), was on a winning streak, going on for the past seven Delta Cycles. She had recently defeated Phoenix Clarke, Gen Epsilon, Lieutenant of Platoon ♀ (Ankh), who also had a winning streak for the past seven Delta Cycles until now. Footage of Ada's battle with Phoenix gave me a chance to see exactly what other Units beside Blade and Builder could do. Of course the Shield Unit was self-explanatory. The Sniper Unit's symbol was an archer with a single arrow, his bow a translucent electric blue. The arrow was darker and had a shape that appeared electrified, sparking like lightning. This arrow could pierce through enemies and, upon hitting the ground, the Sniper could Teleport straight to the arrow to pick it up armed with a temporary laser field around them. The Thief's hand plates produced an AOE laser field around their hands and themselves. The field around their hands was used to take down opponents. Grabbing them in a choke hold with their left hand on the opponent's head immediately downed them. The laser field that could be projected around them could only be used once every minute. This field allowed the Thief to steal enemy Nodes, and the field was destroyed on capture. Both of these fields produced a translucent sphere which resembled the hexagonal pattern of a Blaze Luminous around the Thief or their hands in the team's color.

———◆———

When I left the mess hall, my Focus directed me in towards my housing unit. When I walked into the medium sized room, I found two beds, a T.V., two large dressers, a lamp, and an exhausted Nina Glass staring up at the ceiling.

"Woa, what happened to you?" I asked.

"After that stupid lecture Mendez gave us, all the soldiers and Platoon leaders had a free for all."

"Geez, how'd you do?" I asked.

"I got demolished. I placed nine hundred sixty-seventh."

"Well, that's out of one thousand three hundred twenty-six students. So it's not all bad."

"You want to know who won?"

"Who?"

"Giovanni."

"Our Giovanni?"

"Yup. He was... fast. Like one second he's in front of you, the next you're a cloud of sparks that can't get revived," she explained, running her fingers through her hair.

My mind flashed back to when I first looked at Giovanni's card.

"You'll be able to see how things went next Cycle. They'll show it on the Holo-projector in the mess hall," she said sitting up on her bed. Her ginger red hair was even messier than usual, and her eyes were blank. "You should take a nap. I'm gonna go to the lounge," I said, concerned.

TURN 6.

Lounge

"**O**kay, see ya' kid." Nina said collapsing and lying limp on her bed.

I closed the door behind me and made my way down to the lounge area. On the way down I saw Ryan, accompanied by a cheerful Quinn Stokes. I could tell they were headed to the mess hall because they were following the gold light path. Since I was headed essentially in the complete opposite direction I again avoided interaction with Ryan. I continued following my path to the lounge.

It was a large room. The entire back wall was a massive window allowing a good view of the binary star system of Alpha Centauri. There were small groups of students strewn about the room. Most of them were playing with one of the many board game sets provided, while others were doing group Image Training on their Focuses. There was one student who was watching a match that stood out to me. His bright orange hair clashed obnoxiously against the void of space. He wore an incredibly serious expression on his face that commanded respect. As students walked by him, they pat him on the back and say things like "The Immortal defeated by a Machine," and "You'll get her next time." Each time they did he would seem to grow even more serious. The other students calling him "Immortal" confused me. He definitely had a good reputation, and something happened during one of the more recent games. He soon noticed me staring at him so I shot my gaze somewhere else. That was when I noticed Giovanni and Emery doing an Image Battle.

———————◆———————

"Hey." I said sitting down in the empty seat next to Giovanni. They didn't respond. Emery had her arms crossed and her facial expression was intense. Then I noticed both her and Giovanni's eyes were closed, they couldn't hear me either. Suddenly Emery erupted with what seemed like playful anger.

"Cheater!" she screamed and pointed at Giovanni.

"I did not cheat. I am simply better than you," he responded with a smug look on his face

Giovanni looked over at me and saluted with perfect form. "Greetings, Lieutenant."

"Hello Giovanni." I saluted back. "I heard you did well in the first skirmish."

"Yes, I got first place."

I looked over at Emery. "How did you do?"

"I was the third one out, thanks to this murderer over here." She shot a death glare over to Giovanni.

"You were the closest one to me. What did you want me to do, not kill you?" Giovanni asked.

"You could've shown some mercy, at least to somebody."

"But the goal was to win! You at least stood a chance."

"I blocked one attack and then *boom*, I have a laser sword through my neck."

"You could have blocked that one."

"Sure," Emery said sarcastically. "Anyway, where's Nina?"

"Oh, she died in the dorm." I joked.

"Oh, man, now I'm happy I didn't last as long as she did."

"Exactly, I did you a favor," Giovanni said jokingly. Emery shocked his arm with her plates and laughed a little. "Anyway, apparently, there's gonna be a game tomorrow."

"Between who?" I asked.

"Nikhil Wood and Scarlet Strong."

"Didn't Nikhil have a game last Cycle?"

"I think so. I hear she's pretty good too."

"I guess they're not giving her a break," Giovanni said standing up.

"Where are you going?" Emery asked.

"To the mess hall to look at the standings again."

"I'll join you," she said standing up.

"I guess I should go check on Nina then," I said, standing up from my seat.

"Farewell, Lieutenant." Giovanni saluted me then walked out the lounge with Emery.

Those two are getting close, I thought to myself while walking toward the exit.

While I was walking through the hallway, I saw the student again. He was running his hands through his hair, walking in the same direction as me. I followed desperately after him but still keeping my distance. I tapped my Focus to scan him and find out his name. He turned around the corner cutting off the scan at 98 percent. I picked up my pace but by the time I made it around the corner, he was gone.

TURN 7.

Nikhil and Scarlet

I opened the door to my room, still distracted by the strange boy I saw at the lounge. Nina was watching a news report from Amestris on the TV.

"Hey," she said. "Apparently Amestris' Viceroy just started a new research thing. There've been a couple riots recently." She looked still a little tired from the skirmish.

"Who's leading the research team?" I asked, plopping down on my bed.

"Some guy named Dimitri," she responded.

"That's interesting," I said. "Never heard of him"

"Me neither."

"Why'd the riots start, though?"

"Some information leaked about Dimitri containing and experimenting on supposed immortal humans, and orichalcum. Everyone is saying this kinda stuff will cause another Fall."

"Glad I don't live there."

"I'm *from* there," Nina said.

"Exactly"

"Aw, shut up." she said, laughing. "So did anything happen at the lounge?"

"I ran into Emery and Giovanni. They told me there was going to be a Sequence game next Cycle."

"Oh cool! Who's it between?" She was wide awake now.

"Nikhil Wood and Scarlet Strong"

"So the first game is with upper-classmen, huh?"

"I guess so, but I hear Nikhil is really good," I told her.

"What about Scarlet?"

"Not really sure." I checked the time on my Focus. "Oh, crap, we should probably go to bed, it's 1037"

"So? You have a bedtime, kid?"

"No," I said a little embarrassed. "I just don't want the Majors to wake us up super early and we're still tired."

"Alright, kid, you can go to bed now. I'll get ready after you."

"I still think I'm a little bit older than you," I said while walking to the bathroom.

"Remember what I said in the Gen Building?" she said smugly.

"I know: 'Don't know, don't care,'" I said as I shut the door behind me.

———— ◆ ————

My Focus woke me up at around 0600 like it usually did. Nina was still lying limp in her bed. Her Focus had gone off many times, and was still going from what I could tell. I shook her awake just so I could give her the "I told you so" look. Her hair was still as messy as it was last Cycle, and her eyes gave me an annoyed, tired expression.

"Mornin'," I said.

She collapsed back into her bed.

"You're going to wake up whether you like it or not," I told her.

"No," she whined.

"I'll just carry you, then."

"Cool, that mean I won't have to walk."

I picked her up on my back and carried her to the bathroom. She was warm, and I could feel her breathing on my back. Upon arriving at the bathroom I dropped her on the floor to fully wake her up.

"Oww! What was that for?!" she yelled as she stood up.

"That was to wake you up. Now get ready."

"Jerk," she said under her breath reaching for her toothbrush.

———◆———

We walked down to the mess hall for breakfast. We were soon joined by Giovanni, Emery, Eric, and Dayami. Together we spoke over our breakfasts until we were directed to our respective classes.

Most of mine were centered around Strategic Training, as I was a Lieutenant. They mostly dealt with basic strategies for Sequence and watching some of the greatest recorded matches. Also, to remind us of the tragedy that was Earth, we briefly touched on the failures of the Conspiracy War, and how badly the situation was handled, though any questions on what the Conspiracy War was about were quickly but subtly shut down. We were told about the weapon that gave the war its name, CONSPIRE. It was powered by a reaction between anti-matter and orichalcum, a violent reaction that was controlled by the amount of orichalcum in the Reactor. Any further questions asked he would change the subject; gently shifting us back to our training, then our instructor put up the recorded game between Phoenix and Ada.

Phoenix's formation was centered around a spearhead that would plow through enemy forces and eliminate the Lieutenant. Guarded on the sides by Shields and Thieves, with the Blade Units driving the middle, he was reckless, and sometimes even charged into battle himself, gaining Phoenix the title of the greatest offensive leader in the game. His goal this game was clear: to eliminate Lieutenant Ada. If she was downed then all of her forces go with her.

The only problem was that Ada was the complete opposite of Phoenix. Her formation was a perfect defense. Her front line was built of Shield Units reinforced by Snipers, which demolished the advancing spearhead, pushing forward like a wall of death. I didn't notice how Phoenix had his Units moving to encircle Ada's until I saw her right and left flanks move to meet them. I soon noticed that Phoenix had a small group of Thieves moving in toward Ada's Command Tower. Suddenly, four blue walls formed a square around the advancing Thieves. The square closed in and eliminated them all in one go. Ada's defense was unbeatable. She used the confusion of the battle on the flanks to move some of her Blade Units into Phoenix's Tower in secret. It was only a minute after that all of Phoenix's Units dissipated into a vortex of neon red. Ada used his own tactic against him, and after that victory she became the greatest Sequence player in the school. Due to her calculated strategy and ability to predict her opponent's next move, she gained the name "Machine."

———◆———

After my classes I met up with Nina and everyone else for lunch. We each were anticipating the coming game in a couple hours.

"I'm kinda worried for Nikhil," Eric said, starting up a conversation. "Apparently Scarlet stood a chance against Phoenix last season."

"Nikhil has the best builder squadron though." said Emery, looking up from her Holo-projector.

"But Phoenix is second best in the school. He used to be top rank at one point too."

"So? Builders basically control the entire map. If you control the map, you control your opponent."

"But if Scarlet could defend herself against Phoenix, she could easily defend herself against Nikhil's builders."

"Phoenix's main attacking forces are his Blade and Thief Units," I interjected.

"Exactly!" Emery agreed.

"Alright, let's make a bet," Eric said confidently.

"Bet what?" I asked.

"I don't know... If Scarlet wins I get to draw something stupid on your faces."

"And if Nikhil wins, you have to eat a spoonful of cinnamon during dinner," Nina jumped in.

"Perfect." Emery agreed again.

"Deal!" Eric declared and shook hands with Emery.

Time flew by and the game was about to begin. We walked down an ark bridge overlooking the Glass Nebula into the darkness. The stadium was a massive glass sphere suspended above the main Typlar Gate of the Academy. Inside was almost completely dark. The only light was coming from the billions of stars above us. Sitting in its thousands of seats was the entire population of the Sequence Academy, all cheering for one of the two teams. The Hegemony's banner appeared in the center of the playing field. Its appearance alone silenced the multitude of students. Standing in its center was the son of the reigning Hegemon, Selim Bradley, Chief of Hegemony Defenses and overseer of the Sequence.

His powerful almost robotic voice pierced the silence. "Welcome! For those of you who do not know, I am Selim Bradley, son of the current Hegemon."

For a moment he remained motionless in the black triangle of the Hegemony banner. Then he began to walk, and his footsteps echoed through the dead stadium.

"The rules of this game are simple. Eliminate all of your opponent's Units, or eliminate the enemy Lieutenant. Generations Zeta and Epsilon, watch this game carefully. Study their tactics... You never know how useful they will be. Now, let us begin."

Selim warped into the press box and the announcer exploded onto the mic. "Welcome, welcome students! Welcome to the first Sequence match-up of the season! This game we have some leaders who have made good names for themselves up here. On the east side we have the Lieutenant of Platoon ☐ (Asterisk), Nikhil Wood!"

A roar rose from the crowd, and swirling clouds appeared on the field.

"On the west we have the legendary Defier of the Flame, Lieutenant of Platoon ☐ (Rook), Scarlet Strong! And with that said... Let the Sequence begin!"

The farthest east edge of the stadium shone a glorious bright purple as the 50 swirling clouds of neon formed themselves into Units. The same happened on the west, the only difference being that they wore a powerful electric blue. In Nikhil's back line were 20 Builders. At the end of the countdown they built nodes that turned into a wall of rotating X's. Following close behind was Nikhil's Blade and Shield squadron in pairs. Scarlet's Units followed the rotation of the X's and only ten percent were eliminated. Units danced between the X's, slashing at each other. The clash was extraordinary.

Each Blade Unit matched each other, causing sparks to scatter across the pitch black floor. I soon noticed a single Blade Unit darting toward Nikhil's Command Tower, forcing her to call back her Snipers and they took aim on the advancing Unit. It was useless, though, as each shot fired by Nikhil's Snipers was deflected by this single Unit. The Blader almost made it to the tower until he was met by a Thief. The Thief's hands crackled with electricity and formed glowing, sparking spheres around its hands. They both charged at each other. I could tell the Thief was caught off guard by the Blader's speed at first but they quickly adjusted. Their battle captured the attention of everyone in the stadium. They both seemed to be able to predict how each other would move and acted accordingly. Each block sent a sphere of AOE exploding from the center of the clash.

I soon noticed that there were other Blade Units moving in from Scarlet's side to act as reinforcements for the first Blader she sent out. Nikhil noticed too and got her entire Sniper squadron to fire at them only to have them get wiped out by a single Builder. Nikhil's forces were also still struggling on the front lines so they were called back to defend the tower, the Thief managing to slip away in the confusion. Strangely Scarlet didn't continue pushing. She called her Units back, making them form a spearhead. The entire crowd erupted into excitement at the sight of this stolen formation.

"It's like Phoenix!" I yelled.

Nikhil had all of her Units in front of her tower entrance, preparing for the coming onslaught. Her entire frontline was built of her remaining Shield Units backed by Bladers. Scarlet's spearhead charged forward seeming like a desperate attempt to end the game. Then a single Sniper stopped. His bow pointed at the glass dome of the tower. Time slowed, and the crowd went silent as the arrow left a burning, electric blue streak arching through the air. The arrow lodged itself in the tower, leaving a crack in the protective glass dome. Then the Sniper flickered and Teleported to his arrow, shattering the dome in the process, revealing a terrified Nikhil. All hope of victory drained from her face as she kneeled down before the Sniper and accepted her fate. The Sniper didn't hesitate to take aim and fire his arrow straight through her Nano-Reactor. Immediately, all of Nikhil's forces dissipated into glorious vortices of neon and the match was over. There was a long pause, then the roar of the crowd flooded the stadium.

"*Wow!*" boomed the announcer. "What a dramatic finish! Scarlet, the great Defier of the Flame, stands as victor!"

Nina tapped me "Looks like Eric won the bet." she pointed to a pissed off Emery who was busy screaming "Goddammit!" into the sky, with Giovanni attempting to calm her down. Scarlet soon exited her tower, moving with strides of confidence. All that I could distinguish of her was her powerful red hair. She stood proudly with her surviving troops, and snatching the mic from the announcer. "My next great victory will be against you Phoenix! I will crush you under my feet so I can move on to Ada." Grinning from ear to ear, she dropped the mic and warped away leaving everyone more determined to see Scarlet win one more time.

TURN 8.

Post Game

After the match everyone was still feeling the rush of such a dramatic battle. Nikhil's Platoon, however, sat on the field, devastated, while Nikhil herself was also nowhere to be seen.

Nina and I walked along with Eric and Dayami following the current made by thousands of excited students, each of them having their own conversations over each other. As we walked, a bright orange flash caught my eye. I saw him again, the boy called 'The Immortal.' He was walking alongside the same group I saw him with in the lounge, saying something about another enemy.

"Hey," Nina said, breaking my concentration. "You're staring."

"Oh, sorry," I said.

"Nah, it's cool. He caught my eye too."

"Really?"

"Yeah, his hair is obnoxious," she joked.

"Haha," I humored her, but she was right.

"Whatcha guys talking about?" Eric jumped in, putting his lanky arms around us.

"Orange hair, up ahead," Nina told him.

"Oh, what about him?"

"Well, Brandon over here was staring at him, and I was too just because of his hair."

"Oh, it is pretty noticeable."

Dayami continued dragging behind, still silent and gazing into space. I felt bad for her, being left out of the conversation, but if she wanted to join in she could. When I looked back, the boy was lost in the river of students, currently making a sharp right for the Teleport Points. Since we had a decent amount of time before dinner Nina and I went back to the housing area. I dropped my stuff down and sat down next to it. Nina flopped onto her bed and turned on the TV.

"Amestrian Viceroy Micah Lamperouge continues his attempts to soothe the protesting unions that have formed after he began supporting research on technology that uses, supposedly, orichalcum as fuel," the news lady reported.

"I still don't trust this… What do you think?" Nina cut in.

Her question caught me off guard. "Oh," I said. "Well I don't know what he plans to use that research for, so I don't exactly know what to think."

I looked at her. She looked helpless. Her arms crossed her chest and her hands held her shoulders.

"I'll be honest with you." she started. "I'm scared of what might happen to my Sector. That kind of research will send Proxima B down the same path as Earth when C.O.N.S.P.I.R.E was developed."

I sat down next to her. "Hey, uh… I think things will be okay. If that research goes bad, Bradley will stop it."

"I hope you're right, kid." She looked up and smiled. "Everything'll be good."

I patted her on the back. "Let's go meet up with the others."

"Alright." She stood up, still a little shaky. "Let's go."

I sent a message to everyone to meet up at the mess hall. Emery, still upset about losing the bet, showed up first with Giovanni. Then Eric arrived. Dayami wasn't with him.

"Where's Dayami?" Emery asked.

"She wanted to stay in and watch what was going on in Amestris."

"Isn't she from Amestris?" Giovanni added.

"I think so… Speaking of that, where are you guys from?"

"I'm from Thebes," said Giovanni.

"I'm from the Capital," said Emery.

"Xerxes," I added.

"Amestris," said Nina.

"And I'm from Mechross."

"So what was that for?" Emery asked.

"I don't know, just getting to know each other better?" Eric shrugged.

"Hey, you still need to punish Emery for losing the bet," Nina chimed in with a smug look.

"Nina, you traitor!" Emery shot Nina a death glare.

"Don't worry, I'll spare you for now, young one, just don't expect me to do this again."

"You better," Emery scowled.

They were playing the ending move of the last game on the Holo-projector when I heard someone slam the table "They used your strategy," a voice behind me said. "I know, I was there," another gruff, annoyed voice responded.

From what the first guy said one of them had to be Phoenix. I turned around, and the person I saw was... the boy from the lounge! *He* was Phoenix, the boy with burning red hair, a powerful build and a short temper. *He* was the one they called the Immortal! His amber eyes were sharp, and filled with drive. He had a Hegemon Wrath tat-too in the center of his forehead, intimidating me even more.

TURN 9.

Skirmish 1
___

Phoenix was visibly upset by Scarlet's challenge to him at the end of the game. The incredible stunt that she pulled to finish off Nikhil sent a message about just how determined she was. I saw one of his friends mouth something I couldn't make out and Phoenix stood up sharply. He grabbed his jacket and walked toward a girl around his same height. She had a powerful stride and an average build. She also wore a Hegemon power tattoo on the back of her right hand. Her prideful grin was unmistakable. They both stood before each other, neither of their expressions changing. "Phoenix Clarke," the girl said.

"Scarlet Strong."

"I just wanted to state my challenge again... in person."

"Go ahead," Phoenix smirked.

"When I face you, I intend to win, then I'll move on to Ada. So you better give me a good game." She extended her hand.

"I will, but don't expect to win. I'll crush you just like everyone else." They shook hands and walked off in opposite directions, leaving me and everyone else who had seen it excited to witness their showdown.

———•———

After dinner the launch groups were able to have our first real training session. I gathered my Platoon in our sub-stadium area. Mine was fairly balanced: ten Thieves, ten Shields, ten Blades, nine Snipers, and ten Builders. They all were in their respective groups with their Squad leaders standing in front of them. I didn't entirely plan out what we would do for our first training exercise. When I got in position before them they all saluted in unison awaiting my commands. I returned their salutes and began my terribly unplanned introduction.

"Hello. For those of you that don't know, I am Brandon Simons, your Lieutenant." I had to think of something to make them do. I could probably just make them have a skirmish with their squadrons to assess their skills, but the problem would be Giovanni.

I said, "Squadron leaders, take your groups to the corners, and wait for further instruction."

I could just separate them, and then before the skirmish I could take Giovanni to observe with me so that everyone would have an even chance.

All the squadrons moved to their areas and had already activated their Nano-Reactors.

"Set your Reactors to separate teams," I ordered, "and your training settings to no revives. Also to help balance this game, I'm going to have Giovanni observe with me in the press box." Giovanni didn't question anything and moved without hesitation.

When we entered the press box, the entire stadium went dark, with the only light being the bright neon colors produced by each of the different squads. The box had a Holo-projector to each of the five corners of the stadium. In the center of the pentagon it said, *Begin*. I tapped it, and the countdown started. When it hit zero a loud buzzer sounded through the stadium and the skirmish began.

The fastest to move were the Shield Units. Eric commanded three of his men to move along the southeastern wall towards the Thieves, who were stationary in their corner. Eric also appeared to be taking the other seven of his men straight across the field to the Snipers. Moving to intercept them were the Bladers, coming in from Eric's right flank. He had made himself an open target. The three Units he had sent towards the Thieves had finally arrived, only to be enveloped by a mob and eliminated. The Blade squadron clashed with the Shields sending red and orange, neon sparks flying across the field. During this clash, Emery commanded her squadron to move in and surround them while they were fighting. The Builders also took advantage. A massive wall moved out from the Builder's corner dividing the entire field in half and eliminating the remaining Shield Units and four of the Bladers. With the Shield Units gone, Dayami sent out her Snipers to eliminate the Thieves who were still moving along the massive wall produced by the Builders. While the Snipers took aim, Emery began to emit a powerful electric current. She and her troops didn't acknowledge the Snipers, or the Bladers that were charging at them. This powerful electric current spiraled and formed a sphere around her, converting the wall the Builders had made into hers. Once the wall was taken, the entire Platoon charged through the wall head on at the Snipers, while the Blade Units were still trapped on the other side. Dayami and her troops fired at the advancing enemy, but eliminated only three in the process. Emery waited by an arrow for one of the Snipers to Teleport to it along with her other troops. When Dayami Teleported to her arrow, Emery grabbed her by the throat, immediately eliminating her and her entire squadron. With the Snipers down the Builders began to move to eliminate the remaining Blade Units. The Builders trapped the six Blade Units with their walls and finished them off.

Emery had seven Units left while the Builders had their full ten.

"Jonah Sheppard," Emery began. "So you're the last person I have to go through."

"I can say the same to you, Forbes." Jonah responded.

"It'd be really nice if you'd let me win this. I do have someone I want to impress."

"Well that sucks, because I do too." He threw up a hand signal to his troops and they sent out a cloud of fast moving segmented walls to disrupt Emery's formation. It worked too perfectly. Emery was forced to scatter her troops to avoid being eliminated. Weaving through the openings, this disruption was all Jonah needed to finish off Emery and her squadron. He threw up the last signal, and another cloud of X's was shot out, eliminating the remaining Units. With everyone except the Builders eliminated, Jonah was the victor.

I thought, *Jonah would have to be at the center of most of my formations now that I knew his squadron was the most valuable.*

I hit the mass revive button on the Holo-projector and warped onto the field with Giovanni at my side.

"Well done, Jonah, leading your team to victory." I extended my hand.

"Thanks," he said blankly and shook my hand, not looking me in the eye.

"Hey Gio!" Emery yelled while charging at Giovanni, hands sparking from her hand plates. Before Giovanni had time to react, Emery had already taken him to the floor and eliminated him. She gave a victorious laugh and marched away from his swirling cloud of neon sparks triumphantly. One of the Blade Units revived him and he was seething.

"What was that?!" Giovanni yelled.

"I told you I'd get you back," Emery said.

"Well, anyway," I announced, "I'll try to get us into a dual training session so we can work on moving as a full Unit. Thank you, and you can all go back to your dorms."

TURN 10.

Protest

Nina arrived back in our dorm room and jumped on to her bed. "Emery spent the entire beginning of the skirmish planning out how we would move," she complained. "And we still lost!"

"Haha," I said. "Well, you were up against builders."

"We could've beat them though," she protested.

"Yeah..." I said sarcastically.

"We could beat them! Anyway, who will we be training with next Cycle?"

I actually hadn't thought that far ahead. "Uhh..."

"You don't know?"

"Look, I could probably get us to work with Platoon B. Their schedule is pretty similar to ours," I mused aloud.

"Alright. As long as you don't look disorganized in front of your Platoon, kid."

"But you're part of my Platoon."

"No, I'm your Pair."

I had never seen her smile so pleasantly.

I said, "Well, uh, I'm gonna try to find out who the Lieutenant of Platoon B is."

"Okay," she said, then turned on the TV to watch what was going on in Amestris again.

The protests against the research seemed to have died down, though Viceroy Micah hasn't said exactly what the purpose of this research was, which raised some suspicion within the Arrival HQ. Nina seemed very invested in the broadcast, and if anything happened that I needed to know about, she would tell me.

I tapped my Focus and searched for Platoon B on the network. Madyson Reese was the Lieutenant. Because that was the only information provided by the network, I would have to message her next Cycle to set up the dual training session. After the broadcast concluded, Nina got up to go get ready for bed, so I concluded it had already grown pretty late. I joined her in preparation and then fell face first onto my bed.

My Focus woke me up around the same time as usual. Nina, surprisingly, was waking up as well, saving me the time of going through the same transaction as last time. Of course her hair was just as disheveled as last Cycle, but she appeared to have had a good sleep.

"Morning kid," she said with a long stretch.

"Morning." I responded standing up.

Immediately upon standing, my Focus buzzed violently.

"Hey what's going on?" Nina asked getting up and walking over to me. As soon as she stood her Focus buzzed with the same notification.

"O- oh my God." she stammered "Oh God." We both read each of our Focuses. The protests in Amestris had spiraled, leaving the Gen Building and Typlar Gate entrance ravaged. Nina's face flooded with terror as the holographic notification scrolled, revealing images of what was left of the bustling streets of Amestris. The police force got involved, killing over 30 people, and leaving around 50 injured; no prisoners were allowed to be taken.

"Hey, you okay?" I asked.

She wasn't.

"A protest becoming a riot? Thirty people killed! Do *you* think I'm okay?" Her expression burned in confused frustration. She fell back down to her bed, dropping her face into her hands. "Look, I just, ugh." She fell over her own words. "At this rate, war could break out, and I wanted to *not* live through a time like that so I wouldn't have to worry about dying in space. That might sound selfish but it's true. And my parents also live in Amestris. I know I didn't spend my life with them, but they're still my parents. If shit gets worse they could be killed. I don't want to deal with the guilt of not even getting to know the people who made me before they die. If that makes sense." It made all too much sense. No one was allowed to be raised by their parents, we are separated at birth to allow for everyone to be raised equally in the Gen Buildings.

She looked at me. Her carefree demeanor was gone, leaving her looking vulnerable, like she was crumbling on the inside. I didn't know what to do. Through my conditioning I knew she would have to harden herself to events like this. This was the first time in a lifetime that a riot in a Sector was even thought of. I tried to speak, to say anything that might possibly lighten her mood, make her think everything would be fine. But I couldn't. I wasn't sure myself. Everything was now in the hands of Hegemon Bradley. All I could do was sit back and watch with her.

We both soon received simultaneous messages on our Focuses. *All attendees and officials assemble in the main stadium.* We walked down to the stadium Teleport Points.

The seats there were cold and stiff. We sat in silence for what felt like an eternity. Then the vision of the Hegemon banner bathed in spotlight beams pierced the darkness. Before it stood the lone, silhouetted figure of Hegemon Bradley, blessed by the rays of his own spotlight. Bradley came before us. His powerful broad shoulders were shrouded by his jet black cape. He also wore a blank mask, just like the one Hegemon Locke wore to hide his identity. It had no features, just a smooth, reflective chrome surface. Bradley stood motionless with his hands behind his back in the center of the banner. As I looked at him I saw the twin swords held on the right and left sides of his belt.

"Attendees!" Bradley started. "I know you are all aware of the violent protest that has started in Amestris." His voice was unnaturally calm. "But there is no need to fear what it may become. As followers of the Hegemony they should be aware of our laws."

My heart dropped at that.

Bradley went on: "If any violent acts are committed during a pro-test against the Viceroy, all persons involved in said protest must be purged." An unsettling bass formed in the Hegemon's voice. "The moment a soldier dons his uniform, he accepts that he may die in it. He also accepts that he may kill in it. Because of the casualties of the riot last Cycle the English Division will be sent to the barracks of Proxima A. Colonel Mendez will head that Division temporarily. This should give you all a good example of what it's like to be a soldier. While you are in these barracks you will be ready to move at a moment's no-tice. If Mendez orders you to move, you will move. Your place in the formation will be indicated by your Focuses. If Mendez orders you to kill, you will kill."

I didn't know what he meant by the "English Division." All I knew was that Viceroy Micah, the man who was keeping secrets even from the Hegemony, was getting military protection.

Call to Arms

Hegemon Bradley warped off the stage, being replaced by Colonel Roy Mendez.

"For you Launchies who don't know," Mendez boomed, "the English Division includes Platoons A through Z. Since you will be relocated to the barracks there will be no more Sequence training. Instead, you will begin training in the art of actual battle."

I looked over at Nina, who sat attentively, and was visibly calmer than back in the dorm. Her elbows rested on her knees with her fingers locked together, partially covering her mouth.

"In the barracks there is only one Teleport Bay, and a single Launch Bay," Mendez continued. "The Teleport Bay will lead to the selected Colonial Spire, the starting point for all our large formations. All thirteen hundred twenty-six of you will move from the main Receival Point to whichever highlighted area in the current formation your individual Focus indicates. Lieutenants, you will move with your Platoons, each of you having a Stun Gun. This weapon, as the name implies, will stun any human target without a Nano-Reactor, leaving the target open for immediate execution."

Nina shifted.

"If you are eliminated," Mendez continued, "whether from physical damage or laser reaction, your Platoon will *not* be eliminated, and revival *will* be allowed. Because the Spires will be the most used mode of transportation for you, if a riot does start those will most likely be targeted for destruction. You are the first and youngest members of the Sequence Academy ever to have to consider moving into battle, so always be on your guard. The battles on Earth were brutal hellscapes, boiling cesspools of the human failures of the era. This all was ended by the first Hegemon. Yet the threat of its revival has showed itself, so be prepared."

And with that, Mendez warped off the field.

———————— ◆ ————————

I had only been at Sequence Academy three Cycles and I was being relocated.

Back at the dorm I began packing my things. I pulled everything that was neatly packed in my drawer out and sat down on the floor to sort them out. Nina sat down too, her back against mine.

"So," she said.

"So?" I responded.

"Why do you think Locke thought it was a good idea to put children in the military against their will?"

"I don't know. No one below the Viceroys know much about him anyway."

I continued to sort my things

"You're no fun," she said, leaning her head back onto my neck.

"You doing okay?" I asked.

"I don't want to kill anyone," she said. "I thought I could serve without worrying about death. But, of course, all this has to happen now. And why don't they send in the older gens?" Her voice gave the smallest trace of helplessness. I had no answer. We were both trapped in the same inescapable vortex.

I didn't know what to say. I wasn't conditioned for this.

"You should start packing," I told her.

"No. I want to sit here for a little longer." Her voice was quiet.

We sat there for a long time.

TURN 12.

Diamond

"Their progress is going as expected. Relocation will begin in three hours and twenty-nine minutes."
"When does he plan on making himself known?"
"That has not been disclosed."
"That's interesting... Well, he better continue with the plan."
"It all relies on the will of the people... Someone has to be the villain."
"Tell me about his progress."
"Subject is soon to activate."
"Now we just need three more."
—CALL ENDED—

My Focus jolted me awake significantly earlier than usual, leaving me unbelievably drowsy. Sitting up in my bed, I saw Nina completely unfazed by the incessant blinking of her Focus. I shook her vigorously in an attempt to wake her. Sitting up slowly, she turned her head towards me, her eyes still not opening. I walked mechanically over to the bathroom to get ready for the Cycle, still partially asleep. I soon woke, and Nina and I got the rest of our things packed into our bags. While we were packing, a notification appeared on my Focus. *"Two hours until barracks launch."* I packed faster to ensure that we would be on time.

We both finished and carried our things down to the Capsule Bay, merging into the massive crowd. The Capsule Bay had a large Blaze Luminous shield that allowed people to see the Capsule suspended over the center motor which created the artificial gravity of the Sequence Academy. The multitude of seats in the large room and the cacophony of the many conversations of the students gave off the feel of an airport, only with a clear view into the galaxy. Thirty minutes later the Capsule arrived.

The pack of children gathered at the entrance to be seated. Nina and I managed to reach a seat together and slept almost the entire flight. Having time to think, I pondered what would happen if we had to intervene in a violent protest. It was inevitable, especially with the relocation. The civilians of Amestris now had the threat of the military hanging over their heads, as well as a Government official keeping secrets from them that could potentially lead to another Fall. The Hegemony most likely seemed oppressive to them, I reflected

"Hey," Nina said, once again breaking my concentration. "You good? You look... concerned."

"Oh, I'm fine," I reassured her.

"Cool." She resumed her rest position.

I wasn't fine. I would have to command the deaths of people who were only attempting to make their voices heard to the one who could do something, the people who were helping the one they were actually protesting against. This society built around the will of the people was going against the will of the people.

My thoughts were eventually drowned out by the sound of the hyper-engine cutting off and the magnetic suspender turning on I looked out the window. Outside was a large station, around the size of the Sequence Academy but a little smaller It had the same spinning Ring as the Sequence Academy and the Hegemony banner was projected outside the Connection Block. The Capsule attached to the Block and we were allowed to enter the barracks. The station was one large spinning ring with multiple hallways which converged at the center point, leading me to assume that was the Teleport Bay. The same lighted pathways as the Sequence Academy illuminated the floor, guiding us to a specific location.

Mendez marched ahead of us and we followed diligently. It was clear something was on his mind. He led us to an auditorium quite similar to the one in the Sequence Academy, but before we could even enter he stopped abruptly.

"You are free to go to housing," he said. "I will be inside this room if needed." With that he stepped into the auditorium.

Nina didn't question a single word and proceeded to our housing unit. I did the same. Upon arrival we unpacked our things and just stayed in our unit. The barracks didn't have a lounge or a Sequence field, so there wasn't much to do.

"Hey, you wanna try to meet up with the others?" Nina asked.

"Sure, I guess," I said standing up from my bed.

She tapped her Focus. "Emery's Unit is closest," she said, also standing up.

We left the Unit and Nina led the way to Emery's room. When we arrived we found Giovanni sitting cross legged on his bed and staring angrily at the TV, seemingly ready to attack. Emery lay in front of him, her head draped over the side of the bed, facing the door.

"Hey, guys," Emery greeted us. "How's it going?"

"Pretty boring. How about you?" I responded

"I've been fine, but Gio has been staring down the TV for almost an hour now."

"I am just trying to stay alert," Giovanni insisted "If you had been paying attention you would know there's a protest happening in Amestris right now."

"Really?" Nina asked stepping closer to the TV.

From the TV there came the roll of an explosion. The crowd on the screen began to scream and run away from it in panic. At the base of the expanding cloud of fire of the first bomb, a second went off. Then, out of the smoke, 30 or 40 people dressed in all black came charging forward, some throwing explosives at the surrounding buildings.

Giovanni jumped up from his bed. "This is no riot or protest," he said. "It's a terror attack."

Just then an alarm swelled through the barracks, crushing every room in the jaws of fear. A warning symbol appeared on my Focus along with the single message. *Report to Teleport Bay.* We all looked at each other before sprinting for the Teleports. My Focus gave me a bright yellow arrow on the ground that led to a straight, long hallway. The sound of the alarm blaring in my ears made my head pulse, and each stride matched the swells. The hallway had a red tint to it from the spinning red lights that hung from the ceiling. At the end of the hallway I could see the electric blue diamond of the Spire Teleport Point. Inside the room was my Platoon's alignment area. I stood in front while Giovanni and Emery were behind me and to the right. Nina stood behind Emery forming a single file line. To my left stood Platoon B. Their Lieutenant stood strong and still in front of her Platoon. Her curly hair was a deep jet black, and on her neck she wore the Hegemon Ancestry tattoo proudly.

I hefted my Nano-Reactor from the ground in front of me. It was a large vest with a large cyan reactor that pumped a glowing blue liquid. I dropped its vest over my shoulders, and connected its power core to my wrist. From it a needle injected adrenaline to heighten my senses. Soon the rest of my Platoon joined us in formation, Eric and Dayami behind me to the left, Jonah directly behind.

Mendez warped in front of our Division. "Lieutenants! Access your Focuses and ready your Platoons' weapons in battle mode."

I tapped my Focus and its interface appeared before me. I pressed Battle mode, and my Platoon's weapons sparked to life.

"Lieutenants! Ready your Stun Guns."

I tapped my Focus twice and a small pistol-like weapon manifested itself in my hands. Mendez then sent each Platoon through the Teleport Point.

When I went through, I stood on top of the Spire. The skyline of the city burnt orange, and the wind pushed the smoke into rushing black waves. I looked down at the Amestrian streets, scattered buildings engulfed in flames. The Viceroy Tower was on the other side of the Sector but was still visible and unharmed. A good sign, amidst the chaos.

An area was highlighted on my Focus labeled *Point 7*. I moved down the flight of stairs in the Spire and assumed my position. Once we were in formation Mendez cut on the comms. "Platoons C and A scan over the northeast area and terminate all who engage."

I, and the leader of Platoon A, moved forward, leaving our Snipers and Shields behind to defend the Spire. I moved in front of my Platoon, heading toward a slightly different area than Platoon A. Minutes passed then Lieutenant A got on the Comms "Targets sighted," he said. His location was highlighted on my Focus.

Before I could begin moving there, an explosion flung my Platoon forward and knocked us to the ground. I fired wildly into the smoke, hoping I would hit someone. I stood up and charged headlong into the smoke with some of my Blade Units still unsure what was going on. I eventually heard the spray of gunfire from where Platoon A was, and four of their Units were lost. When I looked over, I was tackled and dragged to the ground by a terrorist. Another explosion went off, and ten of my Units were lost. The explosion rang in my ear, the same sharp piercing sound pounding in my head. The terrorist had his arm pressed against my throat, crushing it under his weight. I pulled my arm up to his head and shot without hesitation. His body flew back shaking and spasming with the pulse. I saw one of the Blade Units finish him off by driving his Blade through his chest. Only then was I able to get a proper look at him. He wore a black bandana around his head which also covered his eyes.

Suddenly Mendez's voice sounded through our comms. "Report back to the Spire, we have some down here."

Running down to the Spire we were sporadically interrupted, each time losing at least one Unit. But the attack didn't seem very organized. There was no apparent formation, no apparent goal. Nothing.

They didn't even seem to be focused on the Spire.

Suddenly, a bright light filled the sky. I looked up, and above the Viceroy Tower was a glowing, diamond-shaped light. From it a single beam shot the base of the tower, engulfing the entire building in flames. The base was blown to bits, and the tower collapsed into a jet black cloud of smoke. The Viceroy Tower had been reduced to ashes.

"Retreat!" Mendez ordered through our comms

But we didn't move. We just stood in awe. "I said fall back!" Mendez repeated.

On command, my Platoon returned to the Spire. The battle was finished in about 30 minutes.

TURN 13.

Call to War

"The first event was a success. Everything is now one step closer."
"Things are moving faster than expected."
"Are you sure the people will make the right choice?"
"We can only hope."
"What about the students?"
—CALL ENDED—

We moved back to the Spire, still trying to comprehend what we just witnessed. The smoke rising from the ashes of the tower began to fill the sky, soot falling like snow, darkening my face. In formation, some soldiers were coughing from the smoke they'd inhaled. Their uniforms were black with soot, and the glow of their Nano-Reactors just barely visible. Mendez stood before us, the Spire behind him completely unharmed. The light of the diamond-shaped Teleport Point was visible even from the ground.

"Soldiers," Mendez started. "I have just informed Hegemon Bradley about the situation. He wants us to return to the Sequence Academy so he can speak with all the attendees. We will return to the barracks and then take the Capsule to the Academy." When he finished he began sending Platoons up individually.

In the Capsule my adrenaline wore off, and I was hit with sudden fatigue.

"You look tired." Giovanni said as he sat down across from me with Emery.

"I know, and this wasn't even a real battle," I responded, looking out the window.

Eric sat down next to Nina and was silent, resting his head on his hand.

"This doesn't make sense." I said.

"What do you mean?" Nina asked.

"All of this is just happening out of the blue. There's no way a real attack like that could have turned out that way. There was no coordination in any of the ambushes they made. Yet they managed to destroy the tower."

"What if it all was a distraction?" Giovanni added. "Considering the weapon that was used, they might not have needed a strong plan. Either way, this could only have been some sort of coup."

"And it must have been planned from a while back," I continued. "Whoever is in control of Amestris next will reveal themselves soon."

"None of you seem concerned that we just killed people," said Emery, her head buried in her hands.

"Look, I don't feel good about it, but it's something that we had to do," Giovanni responded.

"I had to see people get electrocuted to death by *my* hands! I got blood on my face!" Emery exclaimed.

"And I had to stab people to death," Giovanni retorted. "What's your point?"

"It was traumatizing!" Emery argued. "Are you saying you're okay with killing people?"

"If it's my sole job as a soldier? Then no. I follow orders."

Giovanni remained calm. Emery grew progressively more frustrated.

"We're not even a month in and you're saying you're a soldier?" Emery rebutted. "We're kids! We shouldn't be killing people!"

"Are you not aware that even more children fought in the bloodiest war in human history? They would have given anything to fight the battle we just had! This is more than your individual experiences," Giovanni retorted. He looked away, leaving Emery simmering in her seat.

The trip back to the Sequence Academy had a heavy tension that didn't seem to fade. We soon arrived at the Capsule Bay of the Sequence Academy and made our way down to the stadium. Inside, the field that was usually a deep velvet black was glowing blue. Hegemon Bradley stood in the center of the banner watching the thousands of children take their seats. Once everyone was seated, Bradley constructed a chair using his Focus and sat down. There were hundreds of camera people in the pit of the field, eagerly awaiting his words.

"Students," Bradley started. "Soldiers, citizens of Amestris... this Cycle, history was made. For the very first time since the Hegemony's inception, a Viceroy was terminated by their own people. A traumatic event that will leave a scar on this empire for years to come. This act of terrorism calls for an increase of security for all Viceroys and increased surveillance in the Sectors of Proxima B. The damage done to the Sector is now being repaired by recalled Swarm Machines, and action against these terrorists will be made in due time. The one responsible for Viceroy Micah's murder has not been discovered at this moment but hopefully they will be captured and executed before any more damage can be done."

Bradley paused, and before he could continue the screen behind him changed from the Hegemony banner to another one. It looked to be a Thunderbird attempting to escape a diamond prison. After this, the image flashed to a video feed of a man wearing a pitch black mask, with no sort of design on it, much like Bradley's. Behind him stood people wearing the same bandanna I saw during the attack, and black jumpsuits.

"Hello, Bradley," the man in the video began. "We are a union of people that have realized the manipulative and secretive ways of the Hegemony and plan to rise up with the death of Viceroy Micah Lamperouge."

Bradley remained calm and turned to speak to him. "And who

might you be?" Bradley asked.

"I am Damocles. The one responsible for killing Micah and his guard," the man in the video, responded.

"So you are staging a coup?"

"You could say that," Damocles said. "But part of it has already succeeded, I have taken Micah's place as leader of Amestris, most civilians agree with my morals."

"Can you prove this?"

The camera filming Damocles rotated to show what seemed to be the entire population of Amestris wearing Damocles' same uniform.

"How is this possible?" Damocles began once again. "I have been working for years to restore the will of humanity into the Government. To create a world where the people's voice is always heard. The order you gave to mercilessly murder the protesting people of Amestris shows that those with power do not care about those without it. I am the living will of humanity. and I will become Hegemon." I am the driving force that reveals the secrets of the Hegemony. In the Law of the Hegemon war method, I and all of Amestris, declare war."

"You now have the remainder of humanity against you," said Bradley.

"They will join my cause if it means they are heard," stated Damocles.

—TRANSMISSION ENDED—

———————◆———————

The stadium was still. Bradley was still motionless as he faced the screen.

"What do we do now..?" I heard someone ask.

It was Phoenix. He was sitting with his usual friend group but I noticed someone new with him. A stoic girl, with her hair a deep blue. She had an emblem on her arm that I couldn't quite make out.

"Well," I heard Gio say. "I actually don't know what to do."

"It looks like a lot of people don't either," Emery responded.

"Welcome to war, students," Bradley stated.

TURN 14.

Counter Plan

"That was an interesting introduction."
"Indeed."
"So how do you think it will play out?"
"In what regard?"
"The students."
"I don't know, actually."
"Well the first event is fast approaching."
"A lot hinges on the outcome."
"We shall see."
—CALL ENDED—

The relocation was canceled after the revelation of Damocles, and Nina's and my things were returned to Sequence Academy. A Cycle passed and Damocles seemed to not be moving, there being no protests in Amestris nor any transmission from him or his union. Amestris was quiet. A watch team was sent down to attempt to get at least some information. That group was Scarlet's Thief squadron.

I heard Nina's voice seep into my thoughts. "Hey, kid, you were supposed to wake me up." She shook me, and dragged me out of bed. "Morning kid." she said with a smile.

"Morning," I said, and stood up. I tapped my Focus to check the time. When I did, I noticed Dayami watching an open feed of Scarlet's recon. "The recon feed is open?" I asked Nina.

"Apparently," Nina responded. "Dayami has been all over it," She told me.

"That's interesting."

"Yeah, her and Eric have been watching it. You think we should too?"

"It could help with strategic reasoning," I told myself.

"Let's start it up then," Nina said, and jumped back onto her bed.

Before we could access the feed, a message appeared on my Focus. *Damocles movement spotted!* I tapped my Focus to open the feed. It put me into the perspective of Scarlet who was leading the recon. They were moving through a dark tunnel area under Amestris. The only light was shining down from a ramp that seemed to lead out into the silent Amestrian streets. Scarlet directed her team further down the ramp cautiously, only to find a large van with a Focus Network Spire on the platform connected to the back.

"They must be planning to move somewhere..." I heard Scarlet say through the feed. "Where are you headed little guy.." Where could they go? Everywhere else was enemy territory. She tapped her Focus and strands of pulsing nano-machines extended from it connecting to the Network point. Once connected, a flood of images and documents overloaded the Holo-screen of Scarlet's Focus. One of the images was a blueprint. It displayed what seemed to be a weapon, but also a vehicle of some sort.

"Hey kid," called Nina from her side of the room. "You think that was what Micah was researching?"

"It could be," I said, "but for some reason I don't think that's what it is." I wasn't entirely sure what it was.

Scarlet looked through the images and found an assault formation targeting Thebes, the nearest city to Amestris, just a few jumps north. "What is it?" one of her soldiers asked. Just then voices came echoing around the corner.

"It's an attack plan on Thebes." Scarlet responded while saving the images. "We'll need to take all of this back before anyone around here notices." She threw up a hand signal and moved with her squadron through the tower silently. Once out they quickly made their way to the Spire and returned to the barracks. When they arrived the feed ended.

"Well that was interesting..." said Nina.

"It was kinda quick though..." I responded. "I'm gonna capture the image of the attack formation to get a better look at it."

"Well," Nina said, and stood up. "While you do that, I'm gonna go visit Emery and Gio."

"Okay, I'll see you later."

I went through the feed again and stopped at the attack formation. I slid my finger across my Focus to capture the frames. That done, I burned the image into reality with the Nano-constructor.

The formation was a simple yet complex structure. The bulk of Damocles' forces would be coming from the southwest. It had other smaller divisions covering both flanks, but the back was open. In the center was an open space that seemed to be heavily guarded. Something crucial was there! I also noticed a smaller faction that would move in from the southeast, directly from Amestris.

That must be some kind of diversion. I thought to myself. *Such a small group wouldn't cause much damage to Thebes. It doesn't make sense to directly attack a settlement with a Blaze Luminous.*

Blaze Luminous... My mind flashed back to the attack on Amestris.

I jumped up with recognition. *The weapon used to destroy the tower! That must be what is at the center of the main formation!*

———— ♦ ————

It wasn't long before a war room meeting was started and I was called down to contribute.

I entered a large room with the same transparent dome as the stadium, one with a massive Focus projection table. On this table was the purple holographic projection of Thebes. Over it was its green

Blaze Luminous shield and outside was the same formation shown on the attack chart. In comparison to Thebes, Damocles' army was about a third the size. The city would be decimated if they were let through. Its attack force, even without the weapon used in Amestris, could flatten Thebes in six hours.

"Lieutenants," General Garner started. "We are now in possession of Damocles' plan of attack. The time in which this will be executed is still unknown, but having a defense on hand is preferable to not having one." His gaze shifted to the group before him. "We should set up watchtowers on the areas of attack so that we will be more easily alerted on any movement."

"Um..." a younger Lieutenant began. "General, with all due respect... We're children, some of us not even over fifteen."

"I don't care!" Garner barked. "You want to let these people die and bring shame to the Hegemony, because I will not hesitate to snap your neck over my knee to let you join them!" He ruffled his mustache with anger.

The same stoic girl I saw with Phoenix last Cycle was shaking her head with disappointment. She was standing next to Phoenix once again. Her expression was blank and cold, and her eyes seemed to pierce anything she looked at. Her hair flowed like silk, intricate diamond patterns woven into it.

"We should also divide our Units by experience," she said. "Have the English Division counter the forces coming in from the southeast, and the Symbol and Greek divisions counter the forces coming from the north, and the Color Division provide reinforcements." She tapped her Focus and the formation she envisioned manifested itself on the projection table.

"What about the weapon they have?" Phoenix asked.

"It's most likely in the center of the main attack force," The girl responded.

Phoenix mused: "Or it is possible that it is just a distraction. The weapon could be in the frontlines of the smaller attack force. Damocles wants us to assume that it would be part of his main attack so we would focus most of our Units against it so he wouldn't have to struggle when pushing the shield from the southeast. It's possible he did the same thing during the attack on Amestris."

At last I joined in. "Damocles could also know that we have his plans," I said. "If he was able to enter a secure transmission line, he could easily access the live feed that was on this Cycle. He also probably made the southeast formation smaller and gave it the weapon to make up for its size and give each formation equal strength. It would be like being attacked from both sides with equal strength. We should just divide our forces exactly in half to counter this. So whatever side is the distraction will be met with enough force to stop it. It's the safest option."

The room was silent as I tapped my Focus to reveal the formation that was in my head. It looked simple, but also looked impenetrable. I couldn't let this fail.

"Look at that, the kid bested The Machine," Scarlet said. "Nice going. He could probably beat you in Sequence, Ada," she joked, but Ada seemed to take it seriously, and I couldn't tell if I had just made an enemy or an ally. That was *Ada* I had just corrected, and I wasn't even sure if I was correct.

"There's a flaw," Phoenix began. "We still barely understand anything about that weapon they're using. No matter what formation we take, we are still at a huge disadvantage." His eyes were determined to put me in my place.

He's right.... I thought to myself. *To somehow defeat Damocles would require a miracle.*

"Does anyone have a better idea?" I asked, my eyes fixed on Phoenix.

It was false courage, I wouldn't stand a chance against Phoenix alone.

"So far your strategy seems the most effective at countering whatever Damocles throws at us," Scarlet said, defending me. She patted my back.

"Well," General Garner said, "since there don't seem to be any other ideas to be played... all in favor of Brandon's strategy?"

About two thirds of the people in the room raised their hands. Even Ada. Reluctantly of course, but it was still a vote. The other third went for Ada's strategy.

On my way back to my dorm, I felt a sense of triumph, but there was still the tiniest bit of fear left in me. Ada was one of the most influential students, and my idea was chosen over hers.

TURN 15.

An Eye

"**D**amocles is an interesting character, no?"
"What do you mean by that?"
"He is working in ways that are hard to track."
"True. Though the students won't have a problem learning about him."
"How long till the first event?"
"Soon."
"Just remember the goal."
—CALL ENDED—

I opened the door expecting Nina to be there but I remembered that she was at Gio and Emery's dorm. I sat on my bed and lay down on my back, eventually deciding to go through the feed again.

I skipped to the flood of images that appeared on Scarlet's Focus, going through the images one by one. Many were of Micah during his last public speech. Others were images of a dragon, identical to the one on the Hegemony banner. There was one other image of a knight holding his sword to the dragon, ready to slay it, or die trying.

Why are these *here?*

I continued to move through the images and came across the same blueprints I noticed before. I couldn't make out what they said, but I still decided to save it. At some point I must have dozed off because next thing I knew Nina was shaking me vigorously.

"What are you doing?!" I asked still being shaken.

"I just found out that your plan got accepted. That's great!" Nina said, still shaking me.

"Thanks." I responded.

"You've got a lot of pressure on you now. So just don't screw up your own plan, alright?" She gave me a confident smirk while still holding my shoulders. "If it fails then a lot of people die or get enslaved or whatever Damocles wants." She had a joking tone, but what she said was true.

"Yes, I know."

We both sat down on our respective beds and I continued to look through the images.

"What are you doing?" Nina asked.

"Remember the random flood of pictures that showed up on Scarlet's Focus?"

"Yeah."

"I'm looking through all of them to try to find out anything else besides the attack plans."

"Oh, that's smart. How many do you have left?"

"I think one more."

"Tell me what it is when you find it."

I continued my search, and came across the last image. It was of a perfectly symmetrical eye. It had three dots above and below it. Within the iris was the shape of an open gate.

"I uhh, found something?" I announced.

"What is it?" she asked eagerly.

"Come look." I gestured to her.

She walked over to me and looked at the picture. "What the hell is that?" She asked, squinting at the image.

"How am I supposed to know?"

"Well, it has to be important if Damocles saved the image right?"

"I guess so... But why does it even exist?"

"Hey, he'll probably tell us eventually."

A Bird

"**S**hould we really use a method like this? The third outcome could leave it all in ruins."

"Even the third could push Humanity for the better."

"Yes, but more blood will be shed."

"What do you do when there is an evil you cannot defeat by just means? Do you stain your hands with evil to destroy evil? Or do you remain steadfastly just and righteous even if it means surrendering to evil?"

"We shall see the answer in due time."

—CALL ENDED—

The next Cycle went on with preparations to set up watchtowers. Ada led those preparations with Nikhil's Platoon providing the first immediate defense. As soon as it was done, the entire army was called and relocated to the barracks. The relocation required an extra extension to the already massive Capsule, just to contain the entire populous of the Academy.

I walked with Nina to the Boarding area silently along with the other students around us. The only sound in the hallway was the soft chatter of the people who were waiting in their seats for the Capsule to arrive. Passing through the doorway I looked out onto the entire population of the Sequence Academy. It was overwhelming. The banner of the Hegemony was suspended above them, the white dragon's wings encircling the three stars within its empire, sitting within a pool of blood poured from the Earth, watching over its subjects, seeming ready to destroy all who opposed it.

Soon the Capsule arrived allowing us to board. Nina and I received a message from Eric telling us where everyone else was seated. Meeting up with everyone went just as usual. Dayami was quiet and working on something with her Focus. Emery was pestering Gio and Eric was tagging along.

"You know, I wonder why Jonah never sits with us," I said.

"Well, he is kinda distant from us," Giovanni replied. . "All the times we see each other he keeps walking as though I didn't just say 'Hi' to him."

"Yeah, even during our close combat classes he doesn't seem to want to speak to anyone," Nina added.

"He speaks with Dayami, though," Eric joked.

"That's interesting," said Emery. "What do you two talk about, Dayami?"

"I don't think I want to talk about it." Dayami responded not looking up from her Focus.

I could tell she was growing more and more distant from us.

"Anyway," Eric continued. "How do you think the battle's gonna be?" His voice was stressed.

"I don't know. I mean this is like everything Damocles has, right?" asked Emery.

"They're going to have Nano-Reactors," Dayami said.

"How do you know?" I asked.

"There's no way Damocles would risk his entire army being killed by the Hegemony. So he most likely will be using Nano-Reactors," she explained.

"How could they get their hands on Nano-Reactors?" I wondered.

I hadn't even accounted for that in my plan. This would nearly double the force they'd be hitting us with, especially with the possibility of them using the weapon against us, plus the fact that an entire Division of the army had little to no experience. *Agh! We won't stand a chance!* The entire fight would depend on my strategy somehow countering Damocles.

"Oh yeah Brandon," Gio started, "good luck in your talk with Viceroy Cornel."

"That's the Viceroy of Thebes, right?" Emery asked.

"Yeah, I hear she's pretty rough," he responded.

"Everything will go fine," a different voice said, one raspy and arrogant. "Me and Ada will be there too since we had some influence in the plan."

It was Phoenix!

"Where is Ada?" I asked.

"She didn't want to talk with the kid who had the balls to challenge her ideas." Phoenix's voice was passive aggressive when he spoke. "No one in our Gen Group says anything against what she thinks except for me."

"Well is there any particular reason you wanted to speak with me?"

There must be something right?

"When we talk with Cornel, you let *me* handle the things… outside the strategy. Ada will leave directly after the meeting. I'll need you to agree to do that as well."

"Why should I do that?"

There's something they both are hiding.

"Just agree." His voice got deeper. It was obvious he wasn't intimidated by me in the slightest.

"I agree," I said. Reluctantly. "But don't expect me not to find out what it is eventually."

Phoenix stood up. "The Hegemony isn't what it seems, kid." he said as he walked away.

I had finally spoken with one of the most influential students in the Sequence Academy. It can only go up.

TURN 17.

Thebes

"The first interaction was notable."
"He's catching on."
"Yes, and I believe the other candidate is too."
"As do I."
"They will soon be entering the barracks. Do as you will."
—CALL ENDED—

The Capsule finally arrived at the barracks allowing us to gather our things and make our way to the Teleport Bay. We stood in Platoon order, teleporting to Thebes one by one. It took what felt like hours before my Platoon could go through the gate and my legs were killing me, feeling like they could shatter at the slightest tap. I went through and appeared at the base of Thebes' Spire.

It was the same as Amestris', a tall black tower with blue Blaze power rails drawing hexagons up to the glowing diamond that connected it to the barracks. Above us was the greenish tint of the Blaze Luminous surrounding the Sector, and in the distance was Thebes.

Colonel Mendez soon connected to my Focus, and I had to assume to Phoenix's and Ada's as well. "Your escort is arriving in ten seconds," he said. "Move to the highlighted point."

A tall woman wearing a deep red suit appeared in the Teleport

Point in front of Ada, Phoenix and me. "Come with me," she said, as we entered the point, then she quickly teleported away again. We followed her, and found ourselves in a hallway. The walls and ground were sleek, made of reflective black marble, with a long navy blue carpet forming a path. The woman led us down the hallway to a giant steel door. The banner of Thebes hung proudly on each side of it, with its lions facing the door. I looked at the door a little closer, and noticed an eye which was split perfectly by its opening. On the other side stood Viceroy Cornel.

She stood strong before each of us, with both of her swords at her sides. She wore the mark of the Viceroy on her forehead. Inside the upside down triangle was her Hegemon Grace tattoo, making her seem to radiate the light of royalty.

"Riza you are free to go," she said.

Despite her powerful and cold appearance, her voice was strangely warm and comforting.

"Yes my lady." Riza responded, standing and exiting the room.

At last the Viceroy spoke to us.

"So, Lieutenants... Run your strategy by me."

"Of course, my lady," Ada started. "First we will have watchers on the south and southeast ends of the Settlement. We also have the assistance of the Generals residing in the barracks."

The Viceroy signaled me to explain my part of the strategy.

"We will have the entire army divided in half and take formation at the watchpoints to counter enemy forces, my lady" I said. "We will meet Damocles with equal force on both fronts, winning due to our combat training and genetic superiority." I lifted my hand to display the formation.

"From there Lieutenants will work in accordance with their General's orders. This will be Damocles' first defeat." Phoenix explained.

Cornel applauded. "Absolutely marvelous!" she exclaimed. "This rebellion will be crushed like the bugs they are. Daring to challenge the Hegemony!"

With the briefing finished, Phoenix motioned for Ada and me to leave. We followed his orders and exited the room.

"What is he talking to her about?" I asked Ada.

"It's none of your concern, child," she responded not even looking me in the eye. Her response bothered me, she was only a year older.

"Seems like you two are hiding something," I pressed.

"Looks like *they're* hiding something." She glanced at me with a slight smirk. *Even she doesn't know?* I tapped my Focus to connect to Phoenix's.

"What does Damocles want Thebes for?" I heard Phoenix ask through my Focus. "There must be something you have that he wants."

"Also classified," Cornel answered.

"So you know why he wants Thebes!" Phoenix pressured. Cornel remained silent. "You know, if it does form a pattern, I could say that Damocles is only going after Sectors that have Gen Buildings. I mean they house a lot more information besides genetic research." He paused. More information? "There is the main Focus Gate, the Infant Psychology Room. The Immortal Soldier Program. Or... the Atheria?" He paused again and finally got a reaction.

"How... How do you know about that?" Cornel asked sounding as if she were trying to keep her composure.

"Oh I know lots of shit, princess, things that'll make you *not* call security. That's why I'm not afraid to talk to you like this. So if you know what's best for you, you'll answer my questions." I could tell Phoenix had a smirk on his face, there was no way he wouldn't. He knew he had won. Though instead of asking anymore questions, Phoenix left the room and joined me and Ada in the hallway.

"So," Ada started, "how'd it go?"

"I got all the information I needed for now." Phoenix responded. He walked down the hallway ahead of us. Ada's eyes darted over to me for a second before she rushed off to catch up with him. *I can't tell if she knows what's going on or not...* I arrived back with the rest of the army a little after Phoenix and Ada. The watchtowers were about done when I got with my Platoon again.

TURN 18.

Raijin

"The board is set."
"So it can begin at any time?"
"Precisely."
"And the candidates?"
"It will be their chance to show even more promise."
—CALL ENDED—

Three Cycles passed since the conference with Cornel. Damocles had not seemed to be active ever since we set up camp in Thebes. Platoon Ankh, led by Phoenix, was on watch in the north tower. His secret interaction with Cornel still bothered me. *There is something going on outside the war...* I thought to myself. *But what? How does Phoenix know classified information? And he still had his Focus connected. There's no way no one at the Main Gate Monitor's didn't hear what happened...*

"Whatcha thinking about, kid?" Nina slapped me on my shoulder shattering my thought process. We were walking through the hallways of Gio and Emery's housing unit.

"Oh... it's nothing really," I responded, trying to hide what I knew about Phoenix.

She looked at me and squinted a little bit as if trying to read if I was lying. "If you say so, kid," she said and smiled and we continued walking.

When we arrived at Gio and Emery's room Gio was looking at information on the swarm. Currently colonization efforts were going on with the planets orbiting Barnard's Star. With these efforts came the discovery of single celled extraterrestrial life, leading to all colonization attempts being stopped.

"Hey guys," I said, stepping into the room.

"Hey," Emery responded. Nina jumped onto Emery's bed, flopping down with a cushioned thud.

"Damocles has a legitimate plan, right?" Gio asked, catching us all by surprise.

"What do you mean?" Emery asked.

"I mean he did just show up one day and had control of Amestris. Now he wants Thebes. What does he even want to do with Thebes? The people here aren't exactly going to listen to him because they hate him already," Gio explained.

"How are we supposed to know?" Nina said.

"Anyway," Emery joined in. "I'm starting to doubt Damocles will even attack. We have our entire army against his; he knows he would lose."

Suddenly, there was a bright flash on my Focus. It was the order to head to the designated area. Damocles' forces had been spotted. We each looked to the Southeast watchpoint, to face what was only known as The Weapon. We looked out into the dusty outskirts of Thebes, the horizon lined with dingy grey clouds. The only sound besides the wind was the buzz of soldiers warping into position.

The battlefield was silent. Then came the thunderous static of Damocles' army warping onto the field in formation. All of the Amestrian citizens stood in place, wearing sleek black uniforms and bandannas that covered their eyes. We greatly outnumbered them, and in their formation was a large opening, just like the chart had said. There was a moment of dreadful anxiety that welled up in my mind. I could hear my heart pounding in my head, slamming inside, echoing and rattling in my brain. A single gunshot went out with a bang, rolling up and down the field, taking out a member of Platoon A, and starting the battle.

I spoke into my Focus. "My Shields, move to the front and protect your Blades." I shot at anything that moved, running out of the front lines and toward the back.

"They have Nano-Reactors goddammit!" Madyson yelled into the coms. Dayami knew it. I watched the enemy formation and noticed they were not moving much, the opening was still there.

"The enemy is waiting for something," I alerted the others.

"For what?" Gio asked.

"I don't know, but it's a central part of their plan of attack."

Eric blurted out, "Brandon, the other Shields won't hold out for much longer!"

"Alright, Blades and Shields, withdraw." I ordered my Units.

Even as troops backed off the front the enemy didn't advance or change position, only shooting in place. This was an opportunity.

"Lieutenant B and C, Get your available Thieves to escort my Builders to ... These points." I said. *Four corners of the field.*

"Understood." responded Madyson.

"Hold up, why?" Lieutenant C asked.

"What's your name, Lieutenant?" I asked.

"Name's, Lee."

"Well, Lee, I found a way to take out the enemy in one move."

"Alright, if you say so," Lee said.

Madyson's troops grouped up with mine, moving along the left. Lee's were moving on the right.

"All Units, if possible continue pressure, and make sure they don't move." I went behind a pretty big rock to monitor progress and give some kind of guidance.

"Hey all nodes are placed." Jonah announced on the coms.

"Alright, get the others to activate them at the same time." I explained.

The message was given and shortly after, four neon green walls of plasma formed a box around the enemy closing in and eliminating all of them. The cloud of light shimmered as it ascended into the heavens dancing as it went. A roar of victory went out from the battlefield, and I stood up from behind the rock to look at the crowd of rejoicing soldiers.

"Hey, we did it!" Nina exclaimed in the coms.

"Should we go meet up with the rest of the army?" Gio asked.

"Mendez would probably like the support," I explained. "Madyson, Lee, get everyone else ready; we're headed to meet with Mendez."

Wait...

There was whistling. No, it grew to rumbling.

A glowing diamond-shaped light came crashing to the surface, hurling chunks of the land flying into the air. A cloud of dust plumed up from the crater and the light dimmed. From it, a giant shadow rose. It seemed to be shaped like a human. There was a massive ring with glowing spheres rotating along it, emanating a loud pulsing sound, a powerful vibration, paired with the grinding of metal. A horrible chill went down through me. My ears were hot; I could feel my heart pounding in my head and in my chest.

"That's what they were waiting for," said Dayami.

A glowing eye like the one on the Viceroy room's door appeared and blew away the dust cloud. It was a Swarm Machine. The machine stepped forward seeming to rock the entire planet. Nearly knocking me to the floor.

"Protect Thebes at all costs!" Madyson cried out.

The orbs on the ring began to spin faster and faster, with huge crackles and sparks of electricity surrounding the machine. A beam of lightning shot out of each orb converging into one massive bolt, blasting open a small canyon on the battlefield. My heart dropped. *Oh shit...*

"Brandon, what do we do about this?" Eric was panicking. His voice was shaky.

"I don't know. I d-didn't expect a Swarm Machine to be the weapon." I couldn't get any thoughts together. Other troops were screaming in terror. Some were blasted into oblivion by the bolts of lightning, others crushed under the giant. I was a helpless child, crumpled up like paper, hiding behind a rock.

"Lieutenant, half of my Units are out," Gio informed me.

"Dammit!" I yelled.

What should I do? what should I do!? I was helpless. *There should be some way to kill it or disable it or something right?* I tapped my Focus and scanned the machine. *Oh, please come on... Yes, it's called Raijin.* My Focus pulled up a blueprint of the Machine. I had to be quick, every second it was getting closer to Thebes. I found the Raijin's core on the blueprints. *That's it!* I charged out into the battlefield, getting jostled by each earth shattering step the Raijin took. "I think I found a weak spot guys!" I announced into the coms.

"Great where is it?" Emery asked.

"Right on its chest. That pink glowy thing," I explained. I tapped my Focus and marked a spot on the field. "Gio and Dayami, meet me right there ASAP," I ordered.

"Got it," Gio responded.

"Understood," said Dayami.

I ran to the location and found them both standing there. The Raijin was halfway to Thebes' Blaze Luminous and we were the only ones that stood in its way. "Guys, give me your weapons," I told them.

"What? Why?" Gio asked.

"Dammit, just trust me!"

"Fine..." he responded, taking off his Blade Glove and handing it to me. Dayami handed me her Neon Bow. "Thanks. Stay here to catch me," I said running towards the Raijin, each step the machine made throwing me around even more.

This looks good enough. I drew Dayami's bow and took aim at the core. I let the arrow loose, etching it in the core.

"Yes!"

I teleported to it grabbing the small ledge that was above it, holding on for dear life. It burned my hands with steam rising off from them. The movement of the Raijin threw me around and the wind was deafening. A shot of lightning went off, the thunder making my ears ring and feel like they were bleeding.

"Be ready. I'm about to jump!" I shouted in the coms.

I readied Giovanni's Blade in my right hand, and I let go of the ledge. As I fell, I used the Blade to slice through the core, with my body weight carrying it down. As I fell back to the ground, the core crackled and sparked. The air resistance pressed against my chest making it hard to breathe. I soon fell right on top of Giovanni, crushing him, knocking the wind right out of me. "Quick… XCoughX Run!" I commanded to Gio and Dayami.

The Raijin stood still in its tracks small explosions going off sporadically near the core. It soon collapsed face first into the dusty ground defeated. With the battle over I sat down in the dust. "Hey, Colonel, we won."

"The enemy on our side is retreating," Mendez explained., "so you could say we won too. Get everyone over there to head down to the Spire."

"Also, I think I found out what Damocles is after," I said.

The idea made me sick. I vomited.

TURN 19.

The Sword

"**H**e thinks quick."
"**Indeed. Though the other two worked well too.**"
"**He said he figured it out.**"
"**I guess we shall find out if he actually did.**"
—CALL ENDED—

The sun was beginning to set under the Thebes horizon. The broken Swarm Machine stared back at me, feeding the terror of my realization. I was still nauseous despite winning the battle.

Things can only get worse from here.

I looked behind me and noticed that the rest of the army was coming our way. The looks of shock on everyone's face when looking at the Raijin were priceless.

I stood up in the dust and went to meet with Mendez. A small wind blew up the dust, making my nose itch. I walked through the large number of soldiers, my body still jittery with adrenaline but weak at the same time.

I soon found Mendez standing at the center of the army. His face was more serious than it usually was. His jet black hair slowly moved in the wind, lightly reflecting the light from my Nano-Reactor.

"I assume you know what I need to speak with you about sir," I said.

THE MASK OF STRATEGY

"Yeah, I see it lying in the dirt," he responded looking over my shoulder at the Raijin. "I'll inform Bradley about it, see if I can get you a meeting with him."

I looked over Mendez's shoulder and saw Phoenix and Ada watching me. As soon as they noticed they quickly looked away.

"I'll round everyone up and head to the Spire," Mendez continued. "The conference should be okayed when we reach the barracks."

We all were making our way to the Spire, walking in our Platoons.

"Hey." Nina elbowed my arm. "You doing okay? You've been pretty silent."

"Oh, I'm fine. Just got some stuff on my mind," I responded.

"Are you sure? I mean we did just stop something that could have killed everyone in Thebes. That's pretty scary."

"Yeah, I'm fine," I said, continuing to walk.

"Alright, kid." She patted my back gently.

We made it to the Spire and warped up to the Barracks. When my Platoon warped in, Mendez guided me down a long hallway. There was a massive door like the one to Viceroy Cornel's room. This door seemed to be made of the same stuff, but it had twelve eyes surrounding one large triangle with what seemed to be a gate within it.

"Garner, Phoenix and Ada will be in there as well." Mendez informed me.

The huge door crept open revealing a large open room. It had a long crimson red carpet leading to the Hegemon's throne. On the left of the throne stood Phoenix; on the right was Ada. Above the throne was a mural of Earth being split in half with blood spilling out from it, pouring down toward Bradley. He was still wearing his black mask and he sat perfectly still, seeming to show no reaction to my arrival.

I walked down the carpet with Mendez following closing close behind. The air was rigid, I was in the presence of humanity's judge, and executioner. I stood before the throne.

"My leader," I said, taking a knee before Bradley. "As you most likely are aware Damocles is in control of Swarm Machines." I was sweaty.

"And?" Bradley responded, sending a chill through me.

"Well, I believe that is what Damocles is after," I answered.

"Explain."

"Well, Amestris is a Sector that is linked to a Swarm faction. This means he now has control over Amestris' Swarm Machines and he can authorize the recall of those machines, as we saw with the Raijin this Cycle. Thebes is also a Sector connected to a Swarm faction. So I believe that Damocles is going after Sectors that have Swarm links. If he gets all of them, he controls the entire Swarm. If he controls the Swarm, he would force the entire Hegemony into submission."

"And what do you propose to do about this?" Bradley asked.

"What if we attack Amestris?" I asked.

"What do you mean?" said Bradley.

"Amestris has a Swarm link. We destroy that, we beat Damocles," I suggested.

"We could send a Swarm Machine of our own," suggested Phoenix.

"No," Ada corrected him. "Damocles would have a Swarm Machine guarding it. A fight between them would kill everyone on Proxima B, We'd have to send a small group to destroy it from inside."

"Exactly," I agreed. "The other plan would be to just assassinate Damocles and take out everyone related to the rebellion. Which I would say would be a last resort."

"How do we kill only the people related to the rebellion?" Ada asked me.

"We would need to use C.O.N.S.P.I.R.E." I explained.

The mood of the room shifted. Phoenix looked intrigued to hear what else I had to say. Ada stood in sheer disgust at using that weapon again. Hegemon Bradley didn't even seem to be fazed at the thought. He sat calm on his throne, his face still hidden behind his mask, keeping his thoughts out of view.

"As you probably know, C.O.N.S.P.I.R.E. stands for CONtrolled SIngularity REactor, with the P standing for nothing. And yes, it was the one used during the Collapse, the one that killed most of humanity. But if Damocles becomes enough of a threat we will be forced to use it!" I explained.

"I like this." Bradley, responded. "How do you plan to counter the Swarm Machines creating a new link in Amestris?"

"What?"

"After the Amestris link is destroyed there will already be Swarm Machines in the Sector that will construct a new one," Bradley explained.

"Uh—" I hadn't thought of that.

"Why don't we just blow up the factory?" suggested Phoenix.

"That might work. The factory is like what controls the Swarm. If it's destroyed the swarm will shut off," I agreed.

"Along with all colonization attempts," said Ada.

"Are Colonies more important than free will?" asked Phoenix. Ada scolded and turned away from him.

"I'm saying that we can continue to fight until Damocles gets too powerful and if we don't come up with a better idea before then, I say we destroy the Swarm."

"And when do you say he would be too powerful?" Bradley asked.

"When he has control of three Swarm Links," I responded. "We would have until then."

"Why do you say he would be too powerful when he controls three?" Bradley asked.

"He would control a fourth of the Swarm. With that he can destroy planets. He could send more machines than the whole army could even dream of defeating!" I explained.

"Run through a strategy for attacking the Swarm with Mendez and Garner when the time comes," Bradley said. His voice showed the level of interest of a scientist watching mice running through a maze, and slightly echoed in the room. "You show more promise than anticipated. The following events will be even more interesting, won't they? You all are free to return to your usual day. There will be a Sequence game next Cycle. I hope you all enjoy."

With that Bradley dismissed us, and we all walked down the hallway.

"Hey," Phoenix called out from behind me.

"Yeah?" I responded.

"You been paying attention?" he asked me with his amber eyes searching my face like he was trying to read my mind.

"To what?"

"The patterns. You know." He seemed like he wanted a specific answer, but I just didn't know what.

"No I don't think I've noticed any *patterns*."

"Just remember, it's in most controversies that the big secrets are hidden," he told me before turning the corner and heading in the opposite direction of me.

Out of Focus

"He is showing more and more promise by the Cycle." **"How do you think the next event will go?"** **"I might add one in between..."** **—CALL ENDED—**

I was halfway to my housing unit and what Phoenix said was still lingering in my head. *"What patterns should I even be looking for? There doesn't seem to be anything out of the ordinary going on."* I thought back to what Phoenix had said to Cornel. *"I'll need him to explain what all that stuff was. That would at least put us on equal footing when it comes to knowledge."*

I finally made it to the housing unit and found Nina slumped on her bed with the news on. "The attack on Thebes was quickly shut down in what was the fastest battle in human history with the leadership of General Felix Garner. What was the most concerning on one hand was the appearance of a Swarm Machine on the battlefield..." Nina shut off the T.V.

"Hey, kid," she said looking up at me.

"Hey," I responded.

"How'd things go with good ole' Bradley?" she asked.

"Um," I started. "I guess it went well," I responded as I sat down on my bed.

"What do you mean?" She became slightly more intrigued.

"I don't exactly know how things will go from here," I said.

"At least you tried. I'm gonna go to bed, so, good night." She stood up and made her way to the bathroom.

"Look at you, going to bed at a good time."

"Har har," she humored me while getting out her toothbrush.

"I might as well go to bed too."

———————— ◆ ————————

I lay in bed and slowly drifted off to sleep. Seconds passed… Then minutes… Then hours.

I woke up in a white room. But it had no walls. It felt like it was expanding and shrinking at the same time. I felt weightless. But heavy. I was burning, freezing, moving, still, happy, and sad all at once. All I saw was: White. Until I didn't know what color it was. Everything I thought I could rely on to give me a sense of reality was gone. I saw a silhouette. Of someone that I couldn't identify. It looked like me, and Nina, and Eric, and Gio, and Emery, and Dayami, and Ryan, and Quinn, and Cornel, and the news lady, and Bradley. Every single person I had ever known in one single person. Devoid of any sort of color or feature somehow.

"Look at you…. An almost perfect Human…"

The silhouette didn't move. Yet it did.

"You're confused? Let me help with that."

The room suddenly had walls. The ground was solid and the room was warm.

"What is this?" I asked still not comprehending what was going on. All I felt was dread.

"Can't tell you that quite yet."

It had many voices when it spoke, as though all of humanity was speaking through one mouth.

"Who are you?"

"Do you want me to be someone?"

"I don't know."

"Let me help with that."

The eye that was on Cornel and Bradley's door appeared on the silhouette's forehead.

"Look familiar?"

"Yeah…" Fear.

"Expect two other people to talk to you about what We just showed you. The coming events will be very. Very. Interesting."

"What do you mean? What should I call you?"

The silhouette quickly got farther and farther away.

I shot up in my bed steaming.

My sheets were moist from how much I was sweating. It was hard to breathe. The entire right side of my head was in blistering pain. Seething and pulsing with my heart beat.

"*Brandon!*" Nina called out to me from the foot of my bed. I couldn't hear her out my left ear. "Dude, I'm gonna take you to the Infirmary, your eye is bleeding. Like it's *bad*."

"Y-yeah…. Sure." But I couldn't move.

"Goddammit," Nina said. She picked me up carefully and started carrying me to the Infirmary.

"It's gonna be alright."

As she ran, I saw a sign that changed to say, The people I mentioned are in there.

When we made it to the Infirmary, Phoenix and Ada were already there, lying on two of the beds.

"Another one?" asked one of the medics. "Take the Focus off," he called back to the others. He told Nina, "Set him down on the bed and head back to your Unit."

"Wait, I can't just leave him here!" Nina argued back as she set me on the bed

"We can't have you getting in the way, so leave, or I will call security."

"Brandon," she said looking at me. "I'll see you later, alright?"

"Alright," I said as she walked through the door. I still couldn't completely comprehend what I had just experienced.

TURN 21.

Start of a Path

"What was that? What are you doing?"
"Giving them all a push in the right direction."
"How is this going to push them towards anything?"
"How does anything get us anywhere? It takes little instances of intrigue that make someone ask questions. Giving the candidates a question they don't all know the answer to will make them all want to know more. They just needed the right question."
"And that is?"
"Who am I."
—CALL ENDED—

I was still burning and unable to move. One of the medics was removing my Focus. The interaction with the Silhouette was burned into my memory but I wasn't sure if it even really happened. Ada and Phoenix were lying in the other beds. Phoenix seemed to be waiting for the medic to leave, while Ada was looking up into the ceiling. Both of their left eyes were bloodshot. Ada's normally neat, straight hair was ragged and disheveled. We heard the click of the door and the medic finally left, permitting us to speak privately.

"So," Phoenix started. "I assume we're in here for the same

reason?" he asked.

"The Silhouette," I responded. "It said it wanted us to talk." The terror I felt wasn't leaving.

"Did you notice the pattern?" Phoenix asked, slowly sitting up.

"The eye it showed me, what about it is important?"

"It told me not to answer that question," Phoenix said with a smirk. "But let's just say a lot."

"Why did you get me roped into this...?" Ada asked.

"You were always a part of this, Ada," Phoenix responded.

That line alone gave me an idea of a bigger picture. "Part of what?" I asked.

"This entire plan," Phoenix responded.

"What is this 'plan,' though?" I asked.

"What do you think?" Phoenix asked derisively. "Is it normal to have a random guy show up, blow up a Viceroy and say 'Hey, let's have a war!' and then this guy has an entire Sector backing him and serving as his army? Then the Hegemony just says okay and here we are in this huge mess. Damocles doesn't even seem to have any real reason for starting this war in the first place. Neither do the Amestrians. Something is going on behind the scenes and I want to find out what. So far all I know is that Ada, you and I are connected to it, and the names of some projects."

"What projects? You never told me this," said Ada.

"I don't need to tell you anything, Ada. Nevertheless, they are the Main Focus Gate, the Infant Psychology Room, the Immortal Soldier Program, and the Atheria."

What would any of these have to do with the eye or the Silhouette?

"Focus... Focus Gate. They took off our Focuses. It might have something to do with the Focus Gate," announced Ada.

"That's an interesting conclusion."

A shiver fell down my spine, and I jerked upward.

One of the medics was standing in the doorway. His eyes were inky black and his Focus sparking.

"Also I like the name Silhouette... I'll keep it."

"How... are you, what?" I stammered "That's not normal."

"Since you're here," Phoenix said as he stood up, his eye still red. "Are we on the right track?"

"Can't exactly say."

"Why can't you?" Ada said, and stood up as well. "Also, whose side are you on, anyway?" She set her icy glare on the Silhouette.

"I am on the side of Humanity. Pushing us to advance by any means necessary."

"Even war?"

"War breaks Humanity."

Another medic walked in.

"But it also brings Humanity together."

Then they both spoke in unison.

"Uniting people under one common enemy is a good method of bringing peace. But don't assume Damocles is our doing. He could have risen as a man who believed he was the one who would bring change to the Hegemony by establishing a new thing to fear and using it to push humanity to new heights. I may also be using you to stop him, and reward the one who does a place as Hegemon. Think of it as a trial for you three. You see, young Phoenix, your assumption is a possibility. But you will need to find out if it is true. I am simply leading you down a certain path. Find out the truth at the end."

The medics collapsed on the ground, leaving me, Phoenix and Ada dumbfounded.

"I couldn't tell if it was saying I was right or not," Phoenix remarked.

TURN 22.

Starting the Path

"**W**hat are the consequences of starting them on this path?"

"That's what I enjoy about Humanity…"

"What?"

"That there is always something that will remain uncertain."

"That may cause a deviation in the plan that we may never be able to account for."

"It's not like they can hide anything from me. I see everything."

—CALL ENDED—

The medics lay unconscious on the floor with their Focuses still sparking. Phoenix knelt down and looked at their faces.

"Their eyes are back to normal now," he said, looking inquisitively into their unblinking eyes.

I was finally able to move again, so I sat up in my bed. "That was very… unsettling," I said.

"Their Focuses are still sparking, so we know the Silhouette is connected to them somehow," explained Ada.

"So the Focus Gate is the most likely connection we have," I added.

"And if it is connected to the Focus Network, it always knows what we're doing," continued Ada.

"Then we can just take our Focuses off," suggested Phoenix.

"Even then it can watch us through the eyes of other people; it'd be pointless," Ada responded.

Phoenix paused and picked up his Focus from the table next to him. "Well it doesn't seem like it wants to stop us from doing anything, so I say we have nothing to worry about," he said while putting his Focus back on.

"We should still be careful about what we do and who sees," Ada responded, going to get her Focus.

"What are we even going to do now, though?" I asked standing up.

"We should wait until we find out what Sector Damocles is going for next," explained Phoenix. "Then during our own time we can sneak into the Gen Building and find some information."

"How will we even find out what Sector he's aiming for?" I asked.

"We could just watch the Swarm launches," Ada said. "If one launches toward a particular Sector, we know that's where Damocles is going." With her Focus on she seemed to feel somewhat complete, but I could tell she was a little nervous with it on.

"So we have a game plan," said Phoenix, making his way to the exit. "We'll talk about this again when anything important happens."

"Oh great," said Ada under her breath.

"What's wrong?" asked Phoenix.

"I'm playing in the Sequence game this Cycle."

"Ha, I hope it's against Scarlet just so you can lose."

"You're not going to cheer me on?"

"You know why I won't."

TURN 23.

First Surprise

"Well, they have their plan."
"Should we stand in their way?"
"..........No... We just sit back and watch."
"What if they find out things too early?"
"Then we just work around it."
—CALL ENDED—

We each left the Infirmary and went our separate directions. Ada sent out a message on her Focus to her Platoon members while making her way to the stadium. The plan that we had come up with still felt like it wasn't properly thought through, I would have to do my own research on the Gen Buildings in secret to not raise suspicion. Of course there was still the possibility the Silhouette was working against us which would make things even more complicated. I soon made it to my housing unit to find Nina, Emery, Eric, Dayami, and Giovanni all waiting for me. Nina ran up and grabbed me by the shoulders, examining me to see if everything was in order. "You doing alright? How do you feel? What happened?" she blurted.

"I'm fine, it's just I can't see out my left eye as well anymore," I responded.

"Well that's good to hear," joined in Eric. "What exactly happened?"

"I don't really know. I just remember Nina waking me up and saying my eye was bleeding." A bold-faced lie.

"Huh. That's weird," Dayami responded.

"Yeah... it must've been a Focus malfunction," Emery joined in.

Gio was in the middle of an Image Training leaving him unaware of my return. Emery laid his head on her lap. "Also there's gonna be a Sequence game this Cycle."

"Oh yeah, Ada's in it," I responded.

"Already?" Eric asked.

"Yup, she's going against Lee."

"Lee Conway?" I asked.

"Yeah, the poor kid's going to get wrecked."

Gio's Focus blinked a couple times and Emery quickly sat him up right. Gio opened his eyes and shot up to his feet. "Lieutenant. I am sorry for not being fully present at your return." His salute was clean and in perfect form.

"It's okay." I responded.

"What time's the game?" Nina asked.

"I think it's at seven." Emery responded, her ears slightly red.

"If that's the case," Gio said as he sat back down, "I'll keep going with my Image Training."

"Alright, I'll head to the mess hall. I haven't exactly eaten anything," I said turning to head out the door.

———— ◆ ————

Time flew by, and soon it was almost seven. The others and I were making our way down to the stadium surrounded by the swarm of students. Once inside the stadium we found our seats and waited in the darkness for the match to start.

On the field, appeared Selim, standing in the center of the Hegemony banner. "Welcome back students," he said, his voice monotone. "I know you all have won your first battle."

A powerful roar came out from the ignorant students.

"But there have been some things to be concerned about. So in order to boost morale, we have a very special rule set. So with that done, let the Sequence begin."

Selim warped off the field and let the announcer take the show away.

"Welcome students!" the announcer exploded onto the mic. "As Selim said, we have quite the special rule set!"

A white square appeared in the center of the field.

"This is the target," the announcer explained. "You capture this area by having a Unit stand within the border for ten seconds. After it is captured, hold the point until the percent reaches 100 to win. If you lose the target to your opponent, then re-capture it; your percent goes back to where it left off. Eliminating the enemy Lieutenant will also result in a glorious victory. Without any further ado, let's introduce our competitors!"

The east side of the field along with the Command Tower lit up a shimmering orange.

"On the east we have a brand new leader! The Lieutenant of Platoon C, Lee Conway!"

A small cheer came from the English Division to support their own, but the powerful roar that came next put it to shame when the west side of the field sparked to life, glowing a powerful electric blue.

"Now without further delay, I am proud to present our Champion! The living Machine of the Sequence Academy, The slayer of the Immortal... Ada Stephens!"

The crowd erupted into joyous cheers just at Ada's name, and the stadium was flooded with sound.

"We'll see a little more of Ada's skills this Cycle, and hopefully this isn't her last surprise!"

With that, both teams' Units appeared in formation on the field. Lee's was simple: he had his Shields in the front, followed by Blades, then Snipers, Thieves and Builders It was a single block. Ada had each of her Shields paired with a Thief. Her Builders were partnered by Blades, and her Snipers were reinforcements for the front lines. It was clear she would need to be more on the offensive for the first phase of the game.

The center target lit up in white and Lee's Units went charging forward. Ada held her ground, seeming to be waiting for something. When Lee's Units stepped on the target, Ada's Snipers let loose their arrows, cutting through Lee's front line with her other Units charging forward. Her Builders, however, remained in the back, with two of them standing in a corner. Both teams' Shields soon clashed, sending sparks of orange and blue neon dancing on the field. Lee's Units were quickly fought off the target, leaving him with only two thirds of his Units left. Ada's builders in the corner sent out a wall on the north and south edges of the field. Using it as a path, they ran along the wall and made their way to the target. Ada's formation changed once she captured the target. She had her Shields surround the perimeter of the target and had her Blade and Sniper Units standing on the inside. Her builders and thieves were quickly making their way to Lee's Tower. The point was at 50 percent when Ada's Thieves made it unscathed to Lee's Tower. Lee's Units turned into a shimmering cloud of neon only seconds after. She won without losing a single Unit. The match was over in only four minutes.

"Uh," the Announcer stammered. "U-Uh... That's a new record folks! Ada Stephens is our victor!"

The crowd exploded into an echoing cheer. The jumbo screen showed the entrance of Ada's Tower as she stepped out into the light. Her expression was cold and unfeeling as usual, but also burning with determination. She was wearing a dark blue glove that I'd never seen her with before. The Announcer warped down and handed Ada his mic.

"Did you expect anything less..." then she warped off the field, and everyone soon made their way back to their housing areas.

"Poor Lee... I wish Ada at least gave him a chance to fight back," started Nina.

"Well, Ada isn't exactly the type to show mercy," I said opening the door to the room.

TURN 24.

Waiting

"She put on a good show."
"Yes. Hopefully she fares well in the next event.
"A shame the outcome she will produce, though."
"Yes... Just how long before the next event?"
"Not long."
—CALL ENDED—

2/19/142 P.C.W.

A Cycle has passed since Ada, Phoenix and I formed our very rough plan to learn more about the secret Government programs that we are somehow involved in. So far nothing abnormal has occurred. Colonization efforts have been normal and there has been no movement from Damocles himself.

2/20/142 P.C.W.

I decided to look at the blueprints for the Gen Buildings. On the southeast entrance there is the least surveillance. Of course if the Silhouette is helping us then the guards won't pose a threat, but I am still uncertain of what side it's on. I will need to look deeper into what it really is. There should be some kind of information on it. Hopefully.

2/21/142 P.C.W.

"Hey," Nina said as she sat down next to me. "You've been... Uh...busy... lately."

"Oh. Uh, yeah," I barely responded.

"Yeah... Is there something going on?"

"Not right now." A lie.

"Will there be something going on?" She seemed concerned.

"No," I lied again.

"Oh... alright... I'll head to bed. So good night, kid."

"'Night."

2/22/142 P.C.W.

The Silhouette. The more I think about it, the more terrifying it becomes. It's the worst enemy to have, but the best ally. It has control over everything.

2/23/142 P.C.W.

A Swarm Machine has just left the Barnard System and if it doesn't stop at the factory it is making its way to Proxima A. Our plan may need to be put into effect. I informed Ada and Phoenix of this so we are all on the same page. Nina and I haven't really spoken to each other in a while... I should do something about that.

2/24/142 P.C.W.

The Swarm Machine didn't stop at the Factory and we have about four Cycles. I got Phoenix to show Mendez what we found, so everyone is being relocated to the second barracks. After the formations and Battle Strategies were set up, it was waiting in Nina.

"Hello Brandon."

"Dammit, why are you using Nina?" My breathing was inconsistent.

"Because I knew she'd be here when you returned."

"What do you... want?" I felt hot.

"I want to answer one of your questions."

I hesitated. Unsure of what to ask.

"What are you?"

Its empty, soulless, pitch black eyes stared at me through Nina's unconscious body and responded.

"I am one being yet I am multiple. I am everyone and yet

I am no one. I am truth and I am lies. I am the cumulative consciousness of Humanity given physical yet not physical form. I am all and I am nothing. I am many but I am one. I am you. I am me. I am your ally but also your greatest enemy, you see. Every man has in himself the most dangerous traitor of all, and the greatest patriot."

With that Nina fell forward with her Focus still sparking, and smoking. I caught her and laid her to rest in her bed. The nanites would have her Focus fixed in the morning.

2/25/142 P.C.W.

Nina woke in the morning not remembering anything that happened. I spent most of the Cycle with her and the others to make up for not talking with her for so long. That night, the Swarm Machine was within range for us to know exactly where it was headed and its name. It was visible from the lounge. The Titan Machine Atlas was enveloped in a green fireball. Rocketing toward the Mechross Sector of Proxima A. It seemed larger than Raijin. There was also a massive pink light coming from its back, between the propulsion system.

"So that's Atlas," Phoenix said, standing next to me and staring at the machine. "I remember stories of the titan who was forced to hold up the sky as a punishment from Zeus. He was then promoted to watching the pillars that held up the heavens. The ancient world was an interesting place. You know, before the Collapse."

"It's interesting how that was thought of as true at one point," I responded.

"We've got three Cycles... How do you intend to stop it?"

"I don't know."

"We better come up with something before it shows up."

2/26/142 P.C.W.

The relocation is done, so next cycle Phoenix, Ada, and I will have our meeting with Viceroy Davis. Afterward we will make it to the Gen Building. If the Silhouette is on our side, the guards won't stop us... But based on what it told me, it is neither on our side nor against us.

It'll be a coin flip.

TURN 25.

The Infant Room

"The event will soon begin."
"We'll learn much about the candidates from this."
"Indeed."
"Tell me, just how far will you let them go?"
"I'm not entirely sure... It depends on what they discover."
—CALL HOLDING—

My Platoon and I warped down onto the rainy surface of Mechross. The Spire area was almost identical to those on Thebes and Amestris. There were still some people on the streets scurrying for cover from the rain. Atlas was expected to be landing on the western edge of the Sector, so Mendez called everyone to their watch posts. Phoenix, Ada, and I, already knowing the drill, made our way to the waiting point. Our escort was Riza again. Her hair was back in a tight bun giving a clearer view of her face. On her right eye she had her Hegemon loyalty tattoo.

We had warped into a long, black marble hallway. The carpet leading to the door was a deep navy blue. The gigantic grey door that led to Viceroy Davis' room had an eye. The eye the Silhouette showed me.

"So," started Phoenix, "anything we should know before we speak with him?" He looked at Riza. She glared at him, shooting her rage like a bullet.

"Don't act like I don't remember what you did with Cornel," she said, just barely holding back a shout. "Davis won't ask me to leave, so don't try anything." She started walking ahead of us and split open the doors.

Ahead stood Viceroy Davis. He sat with a form which radiated a demand for respect. On his forehead was the mark of the Viceroys. Inside the Triangle was his Hegemon Joy tattoo.

"Hello, hello Lieutenants!" He said with a childish charisma. "You may speak."

"Of course, sir," Ada began. "As you have been informed, the Swarm Machine, Atlas, is making its way towards this Sector. It is expected to land to the west sometime next Cycle, so we have set up watch points in that area."

I picked up the narrative: "Once the Swarm Machine is spotted, it'll take the full force of the Sequence Academy. We will have some soldiers work as distractions, and make an attempt at the core. We will have to react to what the machine does and move accordingly."

Phoenix jumped in: "The core is located on the back of the machine and, based on past experiences, can be destroyed by any Unit weapon," he said.

Viceroy Davis flicked back his golden blonde hair. "Brilliant, just brilliant! Nice to know my Sector is in good hands!"

"Viceroy," started Phoenix. "About your Gen Building." Davis' face stiffened into a serious, icy stare.

"What about it?" Davis asked, looking as if he were attempting to regain his composure.

Phoenix smirked. "The Infant Psychology Room..." he said. "Sound familiar?"

"How?" Davis asked. His face was twisted in an amalgamation of fear, anger and confusion at Phoenix's statement.

"Thanks for confirming that for me, Viceroy," Phoenix said, turning away from Davis and making his way to the door. Ada and I simply followed. Riza watched in disbelief at Phoenix's audacity as we made our exit.

We stepped out of the Viceroy Tower. Looking in the direction of the Gen Building Phoenix asked, "How much time do we have?".

"We have until 0600," Ada answered him.

"Phoenix, what was that back there?" I asked. "You could've gotten us arrested for espionage!"

"I just got Davis to confirm that the Infant Psychology Room is real, and there's some kinda secret around it," he responded. "You're welcome." With that he walked to the Gen Building.

His impulsiveness bothered me, but he was the only reason we were getting anywhere.

We arrived at the building around 1600 so we had about two hours to look around. The southeast entrance of the dome was a single small metal door watched by two guards. Both guards wore visors which hid their eyes with reflective plastic. They also held large assault rifles. None of us were allowed to bring our Nano-Reactors, so if we were shot it would be an actual injury. The guards remained motionless as we approached and I could feel my heartbeat in my head. The air was cold and the rain was pelting me with the wind. One of the guards shifted, making me jump a little, but all he did was open the door. I let loose a sigh of relief knowing the Silhouette was helping us. We could finally relax.

We went through the door and found ourselves in a large, empty conference hall. The stage was barren, as well as the many rows of seats. There were two hallways on either end of the stage.

"Which way?" said Phoenix.

"I feel like the Infant Psychology Room would be near the child area. So..." I pointed to the hallway on the left of the stage "That one!"

We walked down the dark hallway for a decent amount of time before coming to a window. Behind the glass was a brightly lit white room, filled with children sitting at desks competing against an AI in chess, a game I remembered vividly. None of them looked to be over six years old. I felt warm remembering doing the exact same thing.

Ada's cold exterior seemed to melt at the sight. "Nostalgia," she whispered before turning to continue down the hall.

Further down the hall we found another bright room, this one filled with three year-olds, each of them being taught how to use their Focus. It was an adorable sight, children clapping their Focuses in an attempt to activate them, and some showing great prowess. One of the medics had to remove a child's Focus simply because he was hitting it too hard.

The next window we came to showed a work out area. The ages of the subjects looked to be scattered from between four through nine. They were clearly being conditioned to be Units.

We continued down the hallway to a staircase. The air was cold. At the bottom of the stairs, was an even longer, darker hallway that led to a double door. Above the doors there was a purple sign that read, "Infant Room." Phoenix read it aloud. "Do you think that's it?"

"It has to be. There aren't any infants allowed in the Gen Buildings," Ada responded.

"You guys ready?"

"Yeah… what do you think we'll find?" I asked.

"Won't know until we go through," Phoenix answered.

We walked up to the double doors and went through.

Dead ahead was a window. Behind the glass was another blindingly white room that seemed to be padded. Sitting balled up in a corner was a girl with terribly unkempt, black hair. Her clothes were torn and there were deep scratch marks on the walls. Above the window was purple text that read *Subject 1*. Phoenix walked cautiously toward the glass. I followed. Phoenix looked at the girl, then at me. "She's too old to be in a Gen Building," he said.

"Yeah. Apparently she's some kind of test subject," I responded.

Phoenix hesitantly tapped the glass. The girl jumped and looked around frantically before noticing us. Her eyes were a deep crimson red and her skin was pale, almost transparent. She was laughing and crying hysterically as she crawled over to us. "People," she mumbled to herself. "People people people people." She stared at us confused.

"What's your name?" Phoenix asked the girl.

"I'm... One..." Her neck twitched. "Stop!"

"How long have you been here?"

"Huh? I've been here for..." She paused. "Ask Judy."

"Who's Judy?" I asked.

"*I'm* Judy!" she smashed her fists against the glass.

"Calm down... Judy. We just want to know how long you've been in here." I attempted to soothe her, and the ghastly figure slumped down into the floor.

"I don't know. I can't see the sun. Frank says 122 years. When he walks in though."

"That's not possible," Ada interjected.

"Have you eaten anything during that time?" Phoenix asked.

"No, they don't let me eat. They say it's part of the test," the girl responded.

"Do you talk to anyone else besides *them*?"

"I have. Every one."

"*Every* one?" Phoenix asked.

"One, Elro, Angela, Kyle," she responded.

"Where are they? Can you show us?"

"In here." She pointed to a corner. "There's Kyle." She pointed to another corner. "There's Elro." She pointed to yet another corner "There's Angela, and One."

"What planet do you think you're on right now?" I asked.

"I'm on Earth," Judy responded.

I looked over at Phoenix who was staring fascinatedly at the girl, Judy, as if he were watching a rat running through a maze. Ada stood next to him with her face showing concealed sympathy for the immortal woman trapped inside the white padded room.

"I hate it here," Judy said.

"I ca—" I started to say, but was cut off when a voice resonating within my mind shook me to my core.

"You should probably leave. I don't want to have to get involved."

We all looked at each other and then back to Judy.

"And her name's not Judy. Nor One, nor Elro, nor Kyle. It's Laura... Laura Lapis. She was found in the ruins of Earth and presumed to be immortal, so she was brought here for experimentation. So far she does seem to be immortal, and the experiments performed on her have brought forth the Immortal Soldier Program."

"We... We should go," said Phoenix. He turned and started walking towards the exit. Ada and I followed leaving Laura alone in the padded room.

"Where are you going?" Laura asked, but no one answered. "Where are you going!?" she screeched. "Don't leave me here!" she pounded on the glass. "NO! NO! NO! NO!!" She flailed in anger and anguish, lashing at the glass in a desperate attempt at escape. But it was futile. Knowing this, she fell to her knees, sobbing uncontrollably as the door shut behind us, leaving her to the dark depths of her insanity.

TURN 26.

Atlas

"**T**he event is starting soon. It will be quite the interesting display."

"Yes. So what does revealing what we did have to do with the plan?"

"You and everyone else will see in due time. これはとても楽しい時間になります..."

"I'm sorry I didn't catch that last part."

"It will all work out in the end."

—CALL ENDED—

A Cycle passed since we went to the Infant Psychology Room. Laura and her connections to the Immortal Soldier Program were still bothering me. The Silhouette was still hiding information from us and I needed to find out what it is. My Platoon was on watch for Atlas and I was watching satellite feeds of it on my Focus. Nina was doing the same next to me.

"It's kind of scary waiting for this thing to hit the ground." Nina said, looking over at me. "Isn't it?"

"Yeah," I responded, "especially after seeing what Raijin could do."

"Do you think we can even beat it though?" she asked.

"I don't know." I said, and turned back to watch the feed.

"What would happen if we lost...?" Nina asked. But her voice was quiet. She knew what would happen.

"It's not exactly something I'd want to think about," I joked.

———◆———

Our shift was almost over when Atlas entered the atmosphere, giving us only about 15 minutes to take formation. I sent out the warning to Colonel Mendez and he sounded the alarm. Alerted, the populous of the Sequence Academy took their positions in the dusty, almost barren outskirts of Mechross, waiting for the Titan to drop from the heavens. The wind was cold and damp from the previous night's rain. Ada and Phoenix's Platoons stood beside mine, Ada motionless waiting for Atlas. The streets of Mechross were silent as all its citizens either hid in shelters or had evacuated the Sector. Minutes passed. The Titan was enveloped in beautiful flames of its atmospheric entry. They twinkled as each second ticked by, and the titan that held the sky came crashing to the surface. Simply the wind from its landing was enough to knock me off balance.

Atlas rose with the massive cloud of dust with a shimmering purple eye displayed proudly on its chest before it disappeared. Its hands emanated a heavenly green, with a pulsing sound that made the air vibrate.

Mendez's voice cut onto the comms. "Stop it from reaching Mechross at all costs. We can't afford Damocles gaining control of another Sector. Move!"

The entire army charged the machine without hesitation, Mendez's words echoing in my mind. Atlas stepped forward, shaking the Sector with it.

"My Snipers," I commanded in the comms. "break off and provide covering fire."

"Got it," Dayami responded. Phoenix had his Snipers follow suit, as did Scarlet, who brought her Platoon in to move with Phoenix, Ada and me.

Scarlet informed everyone: "Hey, its core is on its back. We'll have to wrap around."

"We know," Ada yelled. "I'll keep my Units back to keep it distracted. Card and Symbol divisions stay with me and keep its attention. Phoenix and Brandon, keep moving to the core."

"Got it," Phoenix and I responded in unison.

There was soon a storm of Sniper arrows flying overhead. Atlas crossed its arms and the vibrating sound grew louder and more powerful. Phoenix and I skidded to a halt, staring in awe at Atlas. It was shining green as it expanded its hands, making the ground shatter and emanate the same glowing green color. The machine soon raised its hands making a glowing chunk of the ground levitate into the air with its movement.

Scarlet screamed in a panic "This is out of control we need to stop this *now*!"

Atlas then moved its hands and tore the floating chunk of rock into pieces and hurled them at the Units on the ground, eradicating some of the Snipers firing at it.

"Goddammit, Phoenix," Ada yelled, "why did you stop? The longer you take the more of a hellscape this fight gets."

"I'm sorry," he said, continuing to run. "It's just that this thing is insane."

Atlas was still distracted by Ada's Platoon, and we were halfway around the machine. It was still flinging massive boulders at the different Platoons attacking it, sending billowing clouds of dust into the air. We soon found ourselves facing the back of Atlas There we stopped.

"How are we even going to get up there?" Phoenix asked.

"Same way I got up there." I looked at Dayami who was already handing me her bow. "We will teleport up there."

"Clever kid," Phoenix patted me on the back and Gio handed me his Blade glove.

"Good luck, Lieutenant," Gio told me before I took aim at the core.

I loosed the arrow, watching it cut through the air before etching itself in the back of the Titan. I warped to it, smacking into the back of Atlas, scrambling for something to grab onto. The core was just slightly above me and I was just barely holding onto a small ledge below it; the vibration of the machine rushing through me. I threw myself up and grabbed on to the top of the core and readied the blade. I drove it in, sending flashes and sparks of electricity flying. I stabbed again and again until the core stopped glowing. The machine vibrated faster and faster until it pulsed one last time, followed by an explosion that flung me back to the ground. Gio and Emery caught me, watching as the machine fell, dead.

A resounding cheer came from those who had survived. Those who were eliminated quickly revived and joined in the celebration. The sun was just starting to set, making the victory somehow feel even more sweet. Nina ran up and slapped me on the back after I stood up. "You did it kid!"

"Thanks." I said, letting out a sigh of relief. No vomit this time! "Too bad Damocles doesn't seem ready to stop with this stuff yet."

"It's interesting how there were none of his soldiers out here," Emery joined in.

"Yeah, that is kinda weird..." I said. "I wonder why." Anxiety flooded back into me at the thought.

"Aw, kid, you're all covered in dust," Nina laughed. She was right, my uniform and face were covered in soot.

"And?" I asked.

"You look horrible."

Phoenix stood back and watched us go on with our silly conversation until Ada ran up, and they made their way back to the Spire. Our mission was a success.

TURN 27.

Perfect

"**H**e is now hated by everyone."
"So we can go into the next half?"
"We will wait. There are some more events I must add in between."
"What will you expect to happen?"
"That's what I like about Humanity."
"What?"
"You're so predictably unpredictable."
—CALL ENDED—

With the battle complete, my body was still feeling the rush from the explosion. *I can't get cocky now. It's only been two Swarm Machines I've taken down.* I thought to myself.

We were making our way back to the Spire and I looked up at the massive buildings that were splitting the sky. The streets of Mechross had grown livelier now that Atlas was destroyed. The air was warm, reminding me of Xerxes. The skyline of Mechross was similar, the only difference being that there was no Blaze Luminous shield, allowing the deep purple night sky to seep into the glowing city. Once we entered the city the people on the streets cheered us on as we made it to the Spire and warped up to the barracks. The industrial walls of the station shattered the warm view of the city I had.

"Students!" Mendez yelled out into the chattering group of children. "You are free to roam around the barracks or head to your housing areas, I don't care which. The Capsule will be taking you back to the Sequence Academy next Cycle. You are dismissed." With that announcement everyone broke off in multiple directions.

I went back to my housing area and Nina joined me. She burst through the door and flopped down on her bed. "We ran for so long and didn't even fight anything!" her voice muffled in her pillow.

"Did you *want* Damocles' soldiers there?" I asked jokingly.

"I mean it would have been more interesting," Nina laughed.

"We fought a giant machine; what else do you want?"

"I don't know."

"I remember when you were terrified by this war."

She turned and looked out the window into space. "I still kinda am."

"You brought up your parents before..." I didn't want to pry, but I also kind of did.

"I... I know. Look, seeing how Damocles has all of Amestris on his side, I know it was their choice to follow him. He isn't doing anything bad to them, I think. So... they're doing fine. Also it's not like they were in my life or anything. No one gets to know their parents... I'm rambling."

"You sure are."

"Shut up. Anyway I'm going to bed, I'm tired." She stood up and started walking in the direction of the bathroom.

"I might as well too." I said, standing up and following her."

———— ◆ ————

I dropped down in my bed, closed my eyes and drifted off into the darkness.

Seconds. Minutes. Hours.

White.

This time there was solid ground. The room had walls and it was cold. Standing in the middle was the same black figure. The Silhouette stared at me without eyes, its voice cutting apart reality and sewing it back together.

"Welcome back Brandon. Did you have fun."

My hands were sweaty and my heart pounding out of fear of the unknown. "Why am I involved in this?"

"It is not just you who is involved in this. It is all of Humanity that is caught up in this struggle."

"Then why are you only speaking to Ada, Phoenix and me?"

"You three are the most important pieces in this. Without you three, this story will never be complete."

"What is this story, then?"

"This story is history. It is my story. It is your story."

"Why does this story need to be written, then?" my pulse was starting to return to normal, but it wouldn't quite slow down.

"Why does mankind need to exist?"

"What?"

"Some things are made for the mere enjoyment of others. Some are made to torment others. With these points in place, Humanity chooses places between these points and determines its own meaning. That's the fun that comes with being Human. You choose who you are."

"That didn't answer my question."

"All Humans have in themselves greatness, but few have the drive to truly act on it... History is the story of great men who are shaped by the society they live in. They have the desire to change it to match their view of perfection. This society is perfect in the eyes of all. Any factor that could influence war has been eliminated. This world has been made perfect. It has been made me."

"If this world is perfect, then why are the infants born with disabilities killed on the spot? Does it support meaningless murder?"

"..."

"If this society is perfect, why is this war even happening?!"

The Silhouette paused.

"My work for today is done... It's nice to see we have made progress. Have a nice day, Brandon."

I shot upright in my bed. I was steaming and sweaty, but other than that I was fine. I couldn't sleep the rest of the night.

TURN 28.

Why

"You said you made progress?"
"Indeed."
"What kind of progress was that? He just seems more confused."
"You seem to be getting too comfortable around me."
"Deepest apologies."
"As long as you remember."
"Of course."
"The questions he asked... will make these next events very, very, interesting."
—CALL ENDED—

All of the Cycle I was tired. The Silhouette was stuck in my mind It was a terrifying thing. Something I couldn't even come close to comprehending was guiding my life down a path I didn't even know the end of.

It said we made progress... What does that even mean?

Nina was walking with me down to the mess hall, slightly ahead of me. Her ginger hair was still messy and all over the place. She never took the time to fix it. She turned and looked at me while walking backwards. "You've been pretty quiet, got something on your mind?"

she asked.

"Huh? Oh, no, it's nothing," I responded.

"If you say so. Anyway, I'm pretty sure the others are nearby; we can sit with them."

"Alright." I tapped my Focus and scanned for them.

———— ♦ ————

Soon enough we found them and just spent our time having random conversations and simply enjoying the food. Time flew by and Nina and I were headed back to our housing unit when I realized I needed to tell Phoenix and Ada the encounter I had with the Silhouette. I sent a message to them and made my way to the lounge. I found them sitting at a small round table in the corner. I walked over and sat down, to brief them on what happened.

"I assume you saw it too?" Phoenix started right when I sat down.

"Yeah, what'd it say to you?" I asked.

"Right when I saw it... it just said 'Immortal Soldier Program.'" He looked over to Ada, as if signaling her to take up the story.

"It just said 'Main Focus Gate,'" Ada said. She looked to me to continue.

"There was a lot of stuff it said to me," I said. "But the best reaction I got from one of my questions was when I asked why the war is going on."

Phoenix shifted forward eagerly. "What did it say?" he asked.

"It just said that we made progress. I'm still not too sure what that meant."

"Damn," Phoenix said. He sat back in disappointment and crossed his arms.

"That question," Ada started. "You're heading in the right direction. There has to be a reason it responded like that."

"Then what do *you* think it means, O' Mighty Machine?" Phoenix joked.

"Stay serious," Ada said. "It said to you the Immortal Soldier

Program, and it said to me Main Focus Gate. What could that mean in connection to what it said to Brandon?" Ada paused to think to herself.

"What is the reason Damocles started this rebellion?" Phoenix asked. "He needs to have some kind of reason."

"He didn't state any in his debut attack," I added.

"What the Silhouette told us are possible reasons!" Ada announced, her monotone voice showing a little more emotion.

"What do you me—oh!" Phoenix caught on.

"The Immortal Soldier Program and the Main Focus Gate might be things that he's after," I explained. "He might be trying to reveal them to the public."

"Exactly" Ada agreed. "The question is what's so important about them..."

"We should run this by Bradley to get a Research License," I explained. "So far we're the only ones that are piecing this together."

"There's no investigators or anything?" Phoenix asked.

"No..." Ada pointed out.

"That's strange... there's also how the Viceroys react to certain things... they're hiding something too."

"So should we tell Bradley?"

"Yes, hopefully he'll give us a Research License." said Ada.

"I still don't trust it." Phoenix stood up and made his way to the door.

TURN 29.

Licensed

"**T**hey are moving down the path you're making for them, but the ending is still unpredictable."

"The ending becomes more and more clear as they progress."

"But this... this route doesn't make sense!"

"It makes perfect sense. They'll uncover something very important and useful on their own."

"But what is that? You're not telling me anything."

"You've changed as the events go on."

"What do you mean?"

"You speak differently, you respond differently... Do you question my methods?"

"..."

"I have it all under control. Yes, this path they're taking is different than the one we predicted, but that's because I interfered. One of them will be victorious, and whoever it is will be the correct outcome."

"Of course..."

—CALL ENDED—

3/3/142 P.C.W.

I woke up this Cycle ready to speak with Bradley. Ada got Colonel Mendez to arrange a conference with him so we'd be able to attempt getting our Research Licenses. When the time came we made our way up with Mendez to Bradley's room. Mendez, remaining silent and keeping his hands behind his back, led us on as the doors to the Hegemon's room opened. Once we entered the room each of us took a knee on the crimson carpet before Bradley. He was motionless. His mask stared back at us, and his voice remained monotone as he asked us, "What do you need?"

"Hegemon Bradley," Ada started. "Since we have been the most efficient at deciphering Damocles' behavior and assembling countermeasures, we would request receiving Research Licenses."

"What would you be using those for."

"Sir, we have noticed that there is no current research team assembled. So, based on our recent merits, we wish to take up the position."

Phoenix was stiff, keeping his eyes locked on Bradley. It was a look I hadn't seen in a long time, the same fiery gaze he had when I first saw him in the lounge.

Bradley said, "The Research License will be a large responsibility, requiring you to find as much information about Damocles as possible, and to put us a move ahead of the enemy. Are you prepared for that?"

We all responded simultaneously. "Yes."

"I feel no need to question your ability and motives."

"Thank you, Hegemon Bradley," Ada said.

"Mendez will update your profiles. Enjoy your newfound powers."

"Thank you for your time." Ada stood up first and we followed, turning our backs on the masked leader of humanity and the Sequence Academy. The massive steel doors closed with an elegant thud, leaving us there to speak alone.

"That was fast..." Ada said.

"Good job out there," Phoenix said, patting Ada on the back.

"My performance is now irrelevant since we have our licenses." She turned her head away from him with her arms stiff at her sides.

"Now we just need to think of what to do next..." I said, drifting into a sea of thought.

"The Viceroy Conference," Phoenix explained. "All the Viceroys will be meeting at the capital, and we'll have some Platoons from the Symbol Division standing guard. If we go with them, we have the right to break off and investigate the Gen Buildings without having to worry about the time."

"That's perfect," Ada responded, beginning to walk towards her housing area.

"Wait... how will we get to go with the Guard Platoons?" I asked.

"We just get on the Capsule; we have our licenses now," she responded.

Phoenix looked over at me after Ada had turned the corner. "You're doing good, kid." He stepped off quickly in pursuit of Ada, and I soon followed to go to my housing area.

3/4/142 P.C.W.

I spent the Cycle studying the layout of the Conference Tower in the capital. Now that I had my Research License I could view the full blueprints. The Viceroys and Bradley would meet at the top floor out of two hundred. One hundred were above ground, while the others were under, with extreme surveillance on every floor except the top. Floor 95 was the most interesting. It had multiple small enclosures and one giant room with a glass wall. The schematics reminded me of the room Laura was in.

3/5/142 P.C.W.

There was one more Cycle before the selected Platoons were relocated to the capital, so I met with Ada and Phoenix to explain to them what I found.

"This..." I said, holding up the Holo-map of the room in my hand and slowly rotating it to give them a better view.

"It *is* just the room that Laura was in..." Phoenix remarked. "We need to check this out as soon as we get there."

"We should check out other places in the Sector too," Ada explained.

"So we have a plan?" I asked.

"A very basic one…"

TURN 30.

A Tower Built on Failures

"**T**his event will yield quite important information."
"This path is still uncertain. We don't know all the outcomes."
"That's exactly why they're taking this path."
"Understood..."
—CALL ENDED—

My Focus woke me at 0400 so I could meet with Phoenix and Ada to catch the Capsule. I forced myself awake and sat up in my bed. Sliding out of my covers, I tiptoed over to Nina, who was lying so still she seemed dead. I shook her until she gave a groan of annoyance.

"What?" she asked, still 90 percent asleep.

"I'm heading out now, so I'll see you around," I responded shaking her gently one last time.

"Alright... I'll see ya' later, kid," she said, before dropping her face back in her pillow.

I stepped back and made my way to the door, glancing back at her before closing it.

———◆———

I met up with Ada and Phoenix in the Capsule Bay. There were about three Platoons already there waiting for the Capsule, which was to arrive in five minutes. Phoenix was downing a cup of coffee to get his energy back up and Ada was sitting next to him looking over the layout of Floor 95.

"Hey," I said, sitting down.

"Sup, kid," Phoenix responded, looking up from his cup of coffee.

"Mendez isn't giving us Nano-Reactors," Ada informed me.

"Why?" I asked.

"He said they're not necessary for us," she explained.

"I guess that makes sense... We probably won't run into anything that'll kill us." *I hope.*

Soon after my arrival the Capsule was ready to load, and we found our seats. The Viceroy Conference Tower was built on Earth's moon, near the Sea of New Hope. The trip was about 30 minutes giving us plenty of time to organize ourselves just that much better. When the Capsule arrived it landed on a wide white platform suspended over a massive body of water and there was a long hovering bridge that led into Sector Zero. The Capital was massive, with buildings cutting the sky with their crowns and the beams of light formed from Teleport Points outlining the heavens. The Sector was quiet, with little pockets of people walking up and down the streets and the Hegemony banner held proudly at the entrance of every building. The Earth was floating above, a sad reminder of the past in the sky. Fragments of the dead planet drifting off into the void. The glowing core of the planet was partially visible, making the pieces look like blood. Just like the dragon on the Hegemony banner, the Conference Tower was having the blood of the Earth poured onto it.

"Wow," Phoenix said, looking up at the dead marble in the sky. "We really started there..."

Ada refused to look at the planet and started walking faster. "We need to get to the tower," she said.

It was a gigantic white building with blue stripes flowing up the sides. A statue of Locke watched over the entrance, holding an eye in his hands. Marble steps led up to the door, with fountains of the clearest water I'd ever seen on either side of the path leading to the entrance. It was a golden double door with the banners of all 56 Sectors on them. The same eye that was in Locke's hands watched them from above. We each put our own hands on the scanner so it would detect our licenses. With that done, the doors opened with a loud and slow creak, revealing the luxurious inner sanctums of the tower.

The carpet was deep royal blue, with black marble floors outside. The walls were white and the ceilings were high, and giant golden chandeliers hung from above. In front of us was a long black desk with a lady behind it. She wore a bright red uniform, with her hair in tight bun on top of her head.

"May I help you?" she asked with a warm but unnatural smile.

"We're looking for an elevator," Phoenix said as he approached the desk.

"Sure thing," the woman said. "It's right over there." Her smile didn't fade, and her bright red lipstick reflected the light back at us.

"Thanks," Phoenix said, and turned, and we followed him to the elevator. The silver doors parted, we stepped inside and scanned our licenses.

"Phoenix, you seem pretty determined this time," I joked a bit.

"That's because I am," he responded. "We have an actual lead this time, and not some stupid assumptions."

Ada put in Floor 95. "He's right," she said. "What we find should be really important." The elevator began its descent.

It stopped with a ding, and opened to a semi-lit hallway. We stepped out into a cold, damp hallway. There was the sound of scratching on the wall, and in the same purple letters, there was a sign that read. *Immortal Room.* Walking forward, our footsteps echoed.

Suddenly out of the silence came a voice. "Who's there?" It was quiet, and shaky.

"Who is it?" another voice asked.

"I don't know, the scientists shouldn't be back yet," the shaky voice replied.

"Hey, we're around the corner!" the second voice yelled.

We quickened our pace and found a room full of cages. Balled up inside the corner of one was a tiny, pale child with black hair. He didn't look up, but the girl in the cage next to his did. She was sitting on the ground. Her hair was brilliant white, and her eyes sad and tired. "Hey, who are you?" she asked. "Why are you here? What's going on?"

"We're going to ask you those questions, alright?" Phoenix said. He knelt down to get on eye level with her.

"Go away..." the small boy whimpered.

"Who's he?" Phoenix asked.

"That's Elro," the girl responded.

I looked over at Ada, who seemed just as stunned as me.

"What's your name?" Phoenix asked the girl.

"I'm Judy," she responded, seeming to get slightly more confused. "Why're your guys looking at me like that?"

"Do you know someone named Laura Lapis?" I asked.

"You know Laura?"

"So you do?"

"Yeah, we were bunker mates before she left."

"Do you know anything about her being immortal?"

"Not much, besides what Frank says."

"Who's Frank?" Phoenix jumped back in.

"He's just the lead scientist here. I don't know much. I've been in this same room for a hundred and ten years."

"How did any of this happen?" I asked.

Judy paused and looked over at Elro. "A couple days before the bunker collapsed," she said, "Laura was taken by some guys and never came back. Then, since I survived the attack in Brazil, they took me to some lab thing, knocked me out then started doing weird stuff to me. Certain things that would kill other people. After a while I caught on that I was immortal, and I met Elro over there, who's going through the same stuff that I am. He's the only reason I'm not insane. I only recently found out about Laura still being alive because she went berserk some days ago."

"Do you know how they made you immortal?"

"I told you, they knocked me out. It might have been some weird procedure thing," she answered.

"We need to find Frank," said Ada.

"Yeah, that seems like the only other place we can get information," Phoenix agreed.

"Wait," Judy said. "Before you go. Why did you even come here, and where are we?"

"You're on Earth's moon, Sector Zero," Ada answered her.

"What?! Why am I on the moon? Why are there Sectors of it? What happened to Earth?"

"That would take a very long time to explain, and we have more stuff to do," Phoenix responded, standing up and starting to walk to the exit.

I stood up and went to follow Phoenix and Ada to the exit. Just before we opened the door there was a notification on my Focus that said *Viceroy Conference begins in three minutes.*

"That's perfect." Phoenix started. "We can question the Viceroys legally for once."

We rushed to the elevator and watched at the entrance floor. Walking front and center was Hegemon Bradley, with Riza and Mendez carrying the Hegemony banner on both sides of him. Behind him followed all 56 Viceroys, separated by system. They all flowed up the stairs to the conference room with a radiant aura.

All one hundred floors were cleared and the conference room doors opened allowing the Viceroys and Bradley to take their seats. The conference room had a massive, clear, round table, with 56 rotating seats around it. There was a large screen and most of the walls were bullet proof glass windows that looked out onto the Capital. Ada Phoenix and I took our seats in a distant corner of the room nearby Platoon (Club). Bradley stood up at the head of the table.

"Welcome, Viceroys" he said. "Thank you all for attending this meeting."

There was a quiet clap that went throughout the room.

"The first threat in a lifetime has finally appeared among us. Introducing to humanity a flaw that never seems to go—"

An explosion went off and shook the entire tower, the bulletproof glass walls somehow shattered just from the tremor. The screen behind Bradley buzzed to life and Damocles was standing behind it.

"Hello again Bradley." The black mask that covered his face was known and hated throughout the entire Hegemony.

"Damocles!"

"You probably shouldn't have all the Viceroys in one area."

Phoenix, Ada and I shot up out of our seats and got out our Stun Guns. I could taste metal in my mouth. The adrenaline was pumping through my system from the first explosion as I pointed my Stun Gun at the door. Suddenly the door exploded sending shards of glass and wood flying and slamming my back into a wall. My ears felt like they were bleeding and the ringing was bouncing around and around in my head. Out of the cloud of smoke stepped Damocles, walking through the fire on the ground before him. A black cape enveloped his shoulders and on his hands he wore white gloves.

"It's just a dumb idea to turn your back on an enemy," he said, reaching for a small black pistol on his waist. There were screams and gunshots coming from the lower levels. I struggled to stand, but my arms were numb and weak. Damocles, without hesitation, put the pistol to his own head.

"If I pull this trigger, I will die and my heart will stop, thus detonating the bomb I have connected to it, killing everyone here. The only way I won't do that is if..." He pointed to the Viceroy of Xerxes. "... You give me the code to the C.O.N.S.P.I.R.E. vault."

TURN 31.

Fear
_____

There were screams of pain and gunshots coming from the lower levels of the tower. The wooden double doors were scorched. Scattered pieces lay strewn on the deep navy blue carpet. The gunshots echoed through the room before being lost to the wind blowing in from the shattered windows. Smoke was visibly rising from the ground surrounding the terrorist hidden in a black mask. It was the same black mask that was hated through the Hegemony, the one that concealed the faces of Viceroy Michah's murderers. It was the one that was now hiding the face of the one threatening to kill the Viceroys along with himself, the one who wanted C.O.N.S.P.I.R.E. Damocles had rocked Humanity with his appearance, and he planned to keep that tremor going until it was an earthquake.

Damocles kept the gun level with his head awaiting a response from the Viceroy of Xerxes.

"What'll it be?" he pressured.

The Viceroy flinched at Damocles' voice. The poor man was terrified. Everything that would happen next, would depend on his answer.

"If you give me the code, we all get to live another day. If you don't, everyone in here dies, and the citizens of Amestris will take hold of the Hegemony in the ensuing chaos."

"I..." Xerxes' Viceroy hesitated.

"Take your time… Think it through." Damocles taunted. "Either way it works out in my favor."

"Just do it… We have no other choice." Viceroy Cornel joined in.

There was a breeze coming in from the shattered window. I managed to pick myself up, but in my hands were tiny shards of glass. Little drops of blood trickled down my arm and splatted on the carpet. Ada was holding herself up against the table, and Phoenix was almost completely unscathed.

Cornel's voice collapsed from helpless despair, to a frustrated confusion. "Just say it goddammit!" She stomped over to him, clutching his collar and jerking herself closer to his face. "I will not let you be the death of me." The radiance she had in Thebes had disappeared.

"Alright…" Viceroy Xerxes gave in. There was no other way. "Alright. It's F-E-A-R."

Fear? Why Fear?

"They do say the most effective way to lead is through fear," Damocles remarked, with a childishly happy tone. "It'll all go smoothly from here," he responded, backing slowly through the door once again. "If you try to capture me before I leave this Sector," he said, "the code was already sent to all my subordinates in Amestris. There'll be no point."

Damocles left the room with his pistol still pointed at his head.

The wind had stopped, my hand was still bleeding, and numb. It had partially dried on my hand, staining it more black than red.

I wasn't afraid. I wasn't panicked. I was helpless. I watched a man be given a weapon designed to tear apart the universe itself with enough power. He was bent on an unknown motive. He was holding the fear of every one right before their eyes, about to unleash its power on them once again. Damocles appeared out of nowhere and started a war, singlehandedly leading an attack that killed a Viceroy. He was a man that shook humanity. The next tremor was on its way.

TURN 32.

Final Moves

"We shall just wait and see how the next events will turn out."
"Yes, but it's even more uncertain."
"Indeed, but it will all be resolved."
"To what extent will this go?"
"How many days does it take to change a society in an efficient manner, and what resources are required?"

The screams had quieted. The fire that was burning the carpet died out and there were wisps of smoke swaying through the air like spiderwebs. Ada was still propping herself up on the table and Phoenix was staring through the door from his corner. The Viceroys were standing, bunched together, behind the Viceroy of Xerxes.

"Goddammit!" a Viceroy screamed and stomped over to him. "It would have been better for us all to die than to have that devil spawn of a weapon be used again!" One of the students restrained her as she sobbed and clawed at Xerxes, streams of her make-up washing away. The playful and happy-go-lucky attitude of Viceroy Davis was gone, and just like Cornel, the radiance and pleasant demeanor had faded.

"What do we do?" Davis asked, looking at Bradley.

Bradley didn't move "We prepare," he responded, still looking straight ahead.

"We won't have time to prepare!" Ada interjected. "Damocles is headed straight for Xerxes!"

"How do you know?" Phoenix asked.

"There's a fleet going there now. My Platoon just picked it up in the satellite room."

"Then what are we gonna do? We don't know how to fly."

"Your Focus will do it for you, you just need to think and it will do." Bradley joined in.

"It's that simple?" I asked.

"Yes. I'll send word to Mendez to ready the Fleet Bay and the students. You all can launch and meet with them at Sector Xerxes."

"We don't have a plan though!" Ada explained. "How can we expect to win if we don't have a plan?"

"Come up with one," Bradley said. "If you don't then Damocles will let out C.O.N.S.P.I.R.E., the weapon that tore apart Earth. Which will it be?" Bradley turned his head to face us, and his mask reflected my face back at me.

There was a pause, filled with our own doubt.

"We'll go to the Spire," I concluded. "We'll at least try..."

I feared a weapon I didn't even know the full power of. It was something I had never even seen in action and yet I knew what it could do. Why now of all times?

I gestured for Ada, Phoenix and the other soldiers that were there to follow me to the Spire, before heading out the door. Outside the bodies of the Amestrians who helped Damocles were strewn about the tower. Even to their dying moments, they wore the mask. But for what?

———— ◆ ————

We made it to the Spire and stood before the massive, spinning, diamond-shaped Teleport Point. "Ada, how long does it take to get to Xerxes?" I asked.

"It'll be six minutes at full speed," she responded.

"Alright." I stepped through the Teleport Point into the barracks. Everyone else followed after, but once through they stopped. All but Phoenix, Ada, and me. Every other student that was with us spazzed wildly for a split second and their Focuses sparked. In front of their faces projected a glowing purple eye, and their eyes became devoid of color and life, before that same voice came out of them.

"Hello again."

"You!" Phoenix said as he stepped toward the group of overtaken students. "Why are you here?"

"I'm wherever there are Humans."

"And what's with that? You keep talking like you're not human. So what the hell are you? I'm getting tired of this."

"I am whatever you want me to be. A force unknown and yet known. I am—"

"That's not an answer," Phoenix said as he stepped closer, his tone getting angrier.

"Stop! We don't know enough about it to challenge it," I interjected.

"When did you start taking control?" Phoenix asked as he spun around. "Last I checked you were a Launchie. I'm the upperclassman and you're the one that's just dragging behind me and Ada."

"What's got your panties in a bunch?" Ada jumped in. "We were all doing fine quite literally a minute ago."

"We just watched a terrorist get the code to use a weapon that caused the Fall! The same guy who doesn't even seem to have a motive. He just walked in and now has enough power to pose a threat. That shit doesn't happen overnight, and I think that thing," Phoenix pointed at the Platoons, "has something to do with it."

"What if Damocles wants to be immortal, or is after something in the Immortal Soldier Program?" I suggested.

"Has it not occurred to you that he controls Amestris? There is an Infant Psychology Room in every Gen Building, so he would have easy access to immortality. Even if that was his goal, he wouldn't need

C.O.N.S.P.I.R.E."

The walls of the room began to slowly crumble. Through the cracks, infinite white. Gravity seemed to fail and temperature was no more. Direction and color and time drifted out of sight as the entire room collapsed into a structured space devoid of everything used to ground reality. In the room was Phoenix, Ada, me, and the **Silhouette.**

"What is this place?" Phoenix asked.

"This is the place where contradiction is truth. Where reality is not bound by reality. A place where I have become eternal. A place where eternity can die. All dependent on Humanity, and Humanity is dependent on me. They always have been for many years."

"Why?" I asked. "Why are you here?"

"Why are you **here? What is the purpose you have made for yourself? Reason and meaning are all too important things to ask another if you haven't even asked yourself."**

"Who are you?" Phoenix asked.

"Who am I? You should find the answer yourself."

"How? What do we even do?" Ada asked.

"Just like a machine to ask for instructions. Cannot even function without a programmer."

"Just give us actual answers!" Phoenix demanded.

"I have given you enough hints already. This world isn't as simple as looking on the surface. Overanalyze, think in outrageous ways. That is the gift you have as Humans, you can look at things and make connections without guidance from an outside force. Look at behavior, symbols hidden in plain sight. Things that seem to be pointless observations. And most importantly, use common sense. If you lose the battle against Damocles now, there will only be one way of defeating him, so play smart. With that said... the endgame has begun."

TURN 33.

Decisive

"They have been turned loose into a world unprotected."
"So the deciding event came earlier..."
"This will show their true skill... the potential hidden away under rules and an outline."
"But... so soon?"
"What better time?"
"What will we do if they fail?"
""
—CALL ENDED—

The other students were unconscious on the ground when Ada, Phoenix and I woke up. The room was quiet. Only the hum of the Teleport Point could be heard.

Phoenix stomped the ground. "Why won't it give us straight answers!?"

"I don't know," I started, "but we don't have time for that. Damocles is on his way to Xerx—"

"YES!" Phoenix exploded. "I KNOW! Dammit, just- We need to get to the ships. Argh I hate this!"

Ada stared at him, confused and sounding defeated. "Phoenix," she said, "you've just been getting angrier and angrier. That won't stop anything."

"Why are you trying to be empathetic?" Phoenix responded. "You don't act like this, why is it different now? You're stoic, and cold. You shouldn't care about any of this and yet you do!"

"I don't know..." Ada collapsed in on herself. "I don't know what to do... I'm scared, and I know you're scared too. I thought if I helped you, you would help me." Her icy exterior shattered. "I don't know what's going on... At first, it was just Swarm Machines and they weren't that bad. But *this?* I don't even know what it *does*... and I'm scared."

"Damocles won't get to use it." I said, stepping closer. "We're gonna go up there, and kill him and everyone else that stands in our way." It was an attempt based in false courage I wasn't sure would succeed.

Phoenix nodded silently.

"Ada, how much time until they reach Xerxes?" I asked.

"Ten minutes..."

The small number of other students that were with us stood up in a daze. Each of them asking, 'What happened?' and 'How did we get here?' Phoenix rallied them together and we started making our way to Fleet Bay.

It was a wide, open hangar. There were ships parked inside yellow squares, each just barely hovering over them. The Launch Gate held the air pressure with a Thompson Field Generator. Beyond it was the endless vacuum of space. We each went to grab our own Nano-Reactors before getting our ships. The ships were hovering white spheres, with a tinted, nano-reinforced glass. Strangely, there were no doors, just a perfectly smooth surface. My Focus outlined the ship and showed a short animation of a stick figure walking and phasing right into the cockpit. I did as instructed. The metal warped around me just enough to get in and sit down in the neon blue chair. There were two circular openings for me to put my arms in, and once I did the cockpit sparked to life and the ship levitated upward.

"Garner did say there was a space part," said Phoenix who had finally calmed down a bit.

"You guys ready?" I asked in the comms.

A unanimous sound went through and they were all battle ready. Seeming to know how I wanted to move, the ship shot forward at a blinding speed, and I was followed by everyone else.

The stars were moving by slowly but we were gunning toward Mars at terrifying speeds. We had six minutes.

Soon enough the planet came into view, and we slowed our engines. Mars looked back at me. Xerxes was visible near a shore, and a small mountain range stood by its side. A tiny forest outlined the Blaze Luminous shield. I should have explored outside the settlement. I flew over to the highlighted area in the formation to join my Platoon. "Welcome to the battlefield. Lieutenant," Gio greeted me.

"Brandon! Nice to see you could join us, kid," said Nina.

"Perfect timing too," I responded. My Focus marked all the enemy ships with red diamonds, and ally ships with blue circles. As they came within range of detection, the number of diamonds grew. We were outnumbered.

"No matter what the odds," Mendez started, "keep them away from Xerxes. If we lose this, all hope is lost."

"Let's give 'em hell!" Scarlet yelled out before zooming out with her Platoon right beside her.

Other Platoons shot out almost immediately after, including mine, firing at every red thing in sight.

"Gio," I called, "take your Units and support back line, some of the enemy is coming in from the right flank."

"Got it."

The void of space lit up with explosions and neon colored plasma. Diving and dodging. Zipping past enemy after enemy. My head felt numb, tingling with every shot. The ship flung out of control from a shot I took on the left. Three were following behind me.

"Someone get them off!" I commanded.

I whipped back around towards Mars and dived for the planet. Shots flying past and just barely missing. With them facing away from the main fight, Nina swooped in along with two other ships gunning them off my tail. We made our way back to the main fight and despite our numbers we had managed to even out the fight. Gio had regrouped while I sent out Emery to cut through with Phoenix. The enemy's numbers had finally dropped below ours.

In the distance, a golden light flickered, then expanded. The tiny light grew into a giant. It was a snake twice the size of Atlas, letting off a golden light from its mouth. A purple eye flashed on its forehead and it fired a continuous beam of light that split our formation in half, destroying every Unit it touched. Damocles' Units swarmed around it and followed as it extended and rocketed for Xerxes.

"Swarm it!" Phoenix cried out, flying with his Platoon at the mechanical python. I ordered my Platoon and we followed suit. Soon the entire Sequence Academy was going to stop the machine. Beam after beam from the serpent reduced our ships to ash. The machine started re-entry when Damocles' ships broke away from it, forming a hexagonal pattern and connecting the points to make a Blaze Luminous. Instinctively I shot at the ships, breaking holes in the shield, allowing me to make it through. Our numbers were dwindling.

"Where is the weak spot on this anyway?" I asked.

"Right in its'... *mouth*?" Phoenix remarked.

"We'll have to fire between beams," Ada concluded. Her Platoon moved in next to ours before swooping near the body of the machine. I scanned it to lock onto the core. *Apophis* was its name, and within its gaping mouth was the core, shooting out bolts of pure energy.

"Eric," I called.

"Yeah?" he responded.

"Group up with Ada, Phoenix and Madyson's ships to lure out a shot from the Machine."

"Are you sure? That doesn't seem like the best thing to do..."

"Just do it."

"Alright."

Apophis was enveloped in a blaze, with its head facing away from the planet. Ada, Phoenix, Eric, and Madyson had their Units within sight of the serpent. Its eyes sparked with golden light and it let out an attack.

"Quick!" I turned up the engines and flew at the beam. Right when it died down, I spun the ship to face the jaws of Apophis. All the other Units in my Platoon fired all the shots we could possibly fire into the beast's mouth. The jaws snapped out of place, the head cracked in half, and through the cracks came streams of light. The body of Apophis shattered and exploded in a chain reaction going from the head, down. Sparks danced through space, falling slowly down to the planet's surface. A resounding cheer of victory went through the comms.

"Well done," Mendez congratulated us. "Looks like we can head down to the planet's surface now."

We took our ships down for a landing a little far out from Xerxes. Apophis was still slightly visible in the bright blue sky.

"We did it, kid!" Nina shook my shoulders back and forth in excitement.

"Just barely," I joked, and shook her back.

"This where you from?" she asked pointing over at Xerxes.

"Yeah."

"Looks nice." She continued to look over at the Sector.

"We won!" Eric ran over and dropped his lanky arm over my shoulder. "And I thought the space part would be harder."

Still looking over at Xerxes, I noticed a flash. A tiny purple light rose up just to the top of the Blaze Luminous shield. It shattered. My heart stopped. I couldn't breathe. The light disappeared, and it grew into a massive void in the fabric of reality. The Spire was ripped apart and pulled into the void. Buildings and the very ground they stood on were ripped to shreds and devoured. The entire Sector was torn from the ground, consumed by the void and condensed into a point of matter smaller than a pinhead. Then the black hole hovered over the crater where Xerxes once stood, before releasing all of its Hawking radiation in a fraction of a second. A beautiful display of catastrophic power. A giant purple blaze of destruction sending a gust of wind and dust, flying at us. I covered my face from the wind and dropped to my knees. My stomach ached, and burned. It was too hard for me to breathe, and my heart was about to fly out of my chest. Nina put her hand on my shoulder, but I couldn't feel it. Xerxes was gone.

TURN 34.

Strings Attached

"**Y**ou didn't answer... So what now?"
"They have one last hope."
"They shouldn't need to depend on that!"
"You seem to forget what I told them."
"I know... it's just... they're kids."
"And?"
"This is happening way too fast for anyone to handle."
"That's exactly why. But right now, we need to give them a moment to be Human."
—CALL ENDED—

The population of the Sequence Academy approached the dusty red crater where Xerxes once stood. The Martian dust clouding the blue sky, darkening it. The buildings were wiped from existence. The streets, Teleport Points, the people simply enjoying their lives, erased. C.O.N.S.P.I.R.E. became the least of my worries. I stood in a cloud of dust, other students running through the crater hoping for the slim chance of finding a survivor. My breathing was heavy, and the dust stung in my chest. I felt a hand grab me on the shoulder.

"Hey." His tone was solemn and broken. "You used to love looking out at the skyline." It was Ryan.

"Yeah."

"You remember that time I brought a stray cat into the room?"

"Yeah."

"And when I brought you outside the settlement for the first time."

"Yeah... I fell into a river."

"You remember when we were first released from our Pod Group?"

"Yeah... I got stuck with you."

Ryan looked out at the dusty, barren, red landscape. "Why'd it have to be here?" he asked. There was no answer. "Come on, let's look for some survivors."

I knew there were none but I decided to look anyway. As I walked, my feet kicked up some dust. My legs were weak, struggling to support the weight of my body, but I looked anyway, my Nano-Reactor was heavy. Mendez soon called us to our ships and we flew back to the Sequence Academy. In the Spire Teleport room, Mendez stood on a podium, looking down at the silent congregation of students before him.

"This... was the turning point," he said. "The most decisive battle. I didn't expect it to come this soon either. Now... with C.O.N.S.P.I.R.E in the hands of the enemy, we have no other options. In this war, we end in defeat. I thank all of you for your service... You are free to return to your housing units."

Mendez turned slowly from the podium and started walking towards the exit.

"Wait!" I yelled out from the silent crowd. "There's one last chance!"

What was I doing?

Mendez looked up and turned to face me with my hand held in the air. "What are you suggesting?"

"Allow me to go speak with Hegemon Bradley next Cycle. It will take some time to prepare." I answered.

I looked over at Phoenix, and then at Ada. "Trust me," I said quietly. Though they really shouldn't have.

Mendez was reluctant, but responded, "Alright. You have one Cycle, and if anything goes wrong it's under your name."

"Thank you, Colonel," I responded, before gesturing for Phoenix and Ada to follow me out the room.

"Good luck, kid," Nina said and smiled at me with what looked like genuine hope.

We exited the room followed by the massive population of students, and made our way to the lounge to discuss our next plan.

"Brandon, what hope do we have?" Phoenix asked. "Xerxes was erased!" It was still a difficult fact to accept.

"I know what happened," my voice choked. "But we have the Silhouette."

"It doesn't even give us direct answers to anything. We'll just end up more confused," Ada responded.

"It said it gave us enough hints and we should be able to find out who or what it is by now. I think if we figure out what it is, it'll give us actual answers," I explained. We needed something.

"Even if we somehow get answers from it, what use will it be?" Ada asked.

"I don't know," I said, "but the Silhouette seems like it wants us to figure out what it is. I mean, it said it gave us enough hints to who it was."

"That is true..." reflected Phoenix.

"So we have a Cycle to figure it out..." Ada's icy glare was lost in thought.

"We need to go back," Phoenix concluded.

"What?" I couldn't tell what he meant.

"The Silhouette said it *gave* us hints already," Phoenix explained. "If we think back to what's happened so far we can figure out who it is."

"That works, but how far back?" I asked.

"Let's say... uh, when Damocles first showed up. That was the starting point for a lot of this."

"That works."

"So, Damocles sends a transmission to the stadium, claiming to be the will of humanity and that he's been working for years to build up a rebellion against the Hegemony," Ada started.

"Wait," Phoenix interrupted. "How did he know we'd be in the stadium?"

"Also, how would he even get the Amestrian people to rebel?" I started. "Racism, classism, sexism—they're gone, the Gen Buildings solved that by raising every child perfectly equal, so there's nothing to rebel against. Unless he's talking about the Immortals."

"Do you think that's why the riots started?" Ada suggested.

"Maybe, but how would Damocles even know about them? The only way we got in without a license was with—" Phoenix paused, and an air of realization flooded the room. "—the Silhouette."

"Do you mean the Silhouette guided Damocles in starting the rebellion?" I asked.

"It's possible," Phoenix admitted. "But if that's true then this entire war is staged."

"That puts us a bit further" I said. "But, agh!" I was collapsing under my own frustration. "That still doesn't tell us by who!"

Ada took control. "Let's just keep running through what's happened. Bradley just... lets us go about our day like nothing happened..." she said.

"So, Bradley also knows something?" I pointed out.

"He might be part of it." Phoenix pulled out a straw and began chewing on it.

"In the Capital," Ada started. "The way he reacted to seeing Damocles was the same as when Damocles first debuted. He didn't even do anything until someone else initiates him."

"After Damocles revealed himself, we had the attack on Thebes," I continued from Ada. "Phoenix, you brought up the four programs to Cornel—"

"Woa, woa. How do you know about that?" Phoenix interrupted me. "You left the room."

"We listened in on our Focuses," Ada admitted.

"Speaking of that, how did *you* know about that stuff, Phoenix?" I asked.

"It was in the feed from Scarlet's group when they snuck into Amestris. I just noticed the names," he explained.

"That's proof Damocles knew about those programs," Ada added.

"So he knows about the Main Focus Gate and the Atheiria," Phoenix added.

"So did Cornel and Davis... What if the other Viceroys know about it?" I suggested.

"Then who's in control?" Phoenix broke in.

"If we know Bradley knows about it... what if he's the one in command?" Ada started. "As Hegemon he could have the power to stage this entire war."

There was a long pause to take in the possibility. The one man sworn to protecting the rights of humanity, was manipulating billions. It was just a game and we were the pieces.

Phoenix snapped the silence like a twig. "Okay," he said. "Am I the only one that noticed the eye symbols all over the place then?"

"No," I said. "But I thought they were just decoration."

"Not just that!" Phoenix started. "They've been at every important location we have. The door to Cornel and Davis room, Bradley's door, and in Locke's hands at the Conference Tower."

"And when a Swarm Machine lands a purple eye shows up in front of them," I added.

"Whenever the Silhouette possess someone their eyes turn black," Ada pointed out.

"And when our eyes were bleeding," Phoenix continued.

"What does that have to do with the Silhouette, though?" I asked.

"When the Silhouette takes over someone, their eyes go black and their Focus sparks. That could mean that the Silhouette is connected to Focus Network and that's how it makes contact us. What if the reason the purple eye shows up in front of a Swarm Machine is that it's being controlled by the Silhouette?" Phoenix concluded.

"If Bradley is the Silhouette, that could explain why he's never involved in our battles. He's working on the opposite side of us," Ada added.

"That's even more proof he's the Silhouette," Phoenix rested his case.

"How did C.O.N.S.P.I.R.E. go off in Xerxes?" I asked.

"Holy shit," Phoenix remarked.

"Even if Damocles' soldiers somehow broke off while we were fighting Apophis, the targeting systems should have noticed," I explained.

"The Silh—I mean Bradley—must have stopped the system from noticing them," said Ada.

"Locke started the Hegemony to give humanity order after the Fall. Now that he's dead I guess stuff like this was inevitable. Why is any of this even happening...?" I was slowly breaking under my frustration.

"We'll finally get an answer to that next Cycle," Phoenix reassured me.

Silhouette

"**D**id you find me? Hidden in the past? A distant memory...? A name uttered only to be hidden? Did you notice me said? Trusted? Watching? Sitting in the blood of the Earth? Waiting to be found... until now? I have made myself known and yet. Unknown. Did you find the hints left? The eye that watches and yet blind? A mind alive and yet...?"

The night was long. I lay there staring at the ceiling, wondering. *Why was so much hidden? Why was any of this happening? How will it end?* It would all be answered soon. I shut my eyes, slowly but surely drifting off to sleep. *It all ends soon.*

My Focus woke me at 0600 like it usually did. Nina was still asleep in her bed but I didn't have the time to wake her. I quickly went to brush my teeth and was out the door. The hallways were silent. No events were planned for this Cycle and neither were any classes, just empty quiet halls. Just in front of the mess hall I found Ada and Phoenix, wearing the same serious expressions they had when we last met.

"You ready?" Phoenix asked. His eyes were strong, knowing that after this we couldn't turn back.

"Are you?" I asked back.

"I'm as ready as I'll ever be" he said "Mendez is waiting for us at Bradley's door. This is our biggest moment."

"Let's head down now," Ada said, stepping off towards Bradley's room.

We walked down the silent halls all the way to Mendez. He stood before the massive door. The same twelve eyes surrounded a triangle, and within that triangle, a lone gate.

"Students. The fate of the Hegemony is in your hands. Whatever way you have found to defeat Damocles will either succeed or fail... but either way, society will never be the same again. Godspeed."

Mendez stepped to the side, allowing us passage into the Hegemon's throne room.

The doors parted as we stepped closer and closer. Through the part in the door sat Bradley, under the Hegemony banner, sitting in the blood of the Earth.

Once in the room, we did not kneel. The doors shut and it was just us and the Hegemon, the man behind the mask was the one pulling the strings.

"You've learned a lot as time has gone by," Bradley spoke through his dark mask.

"We have," Phoenix started. "And it's time for you to help us with something."

"Oh, I know," Bradley responded. "You want answers."

"Exactly, and you're going to give them to us," Phoenix continued.

"Before I can... tell *me* what *you* know." Bradley folded his hands, his white gloves blending into one another.

"This entire war was staged," I started. "You created Damocles, got the Viceroys in on your plan, and set off C.O.N.S.P.I.R.E."

"You've been controlling the Swarm Machines," Ada accused, "and you've been using us to further your agenda."

"But the most important detail..." Phoenix paused for dramatic effect. "You've been using the Silhouette as a mask to do all of it."

Bradley was silent. Hands still folded, he stood up, stepping down from his throne. His heels echoed through the room, rolling up and down the walls. Once on even ground, Bradley raised his hands to his mask. There was a soft click sound, and the back of his mask opened, allowing him to pull the mask off of his face. It revealed a head of slick black hair. His jawline was strong, his features chiseled. But his eyes... His eyes were an endless, deep inky black. Even the whites of his eyes were as black as empty space.

A shiver went up my spine, and my skin felt cold. "All this time?" I asked.

"Ever since he started serving."

"But that doesn't make sense..." Ada said, her face contorted into a look of confusion, and true fear. "If you've been controlling Bradley the whole time then... who are you?"

"Follow me."

The thing that was Bradley turned back toward the throne, the sound of metal scraping against metal rising up from it. The throne itself lifted into the air, suspended by skinny, but strong, steel beams. A staircase was underneath it, and a deep blue light shone from the ceiling of the hallway. Bradley—the Silhouette—walked gracefully, its cape dancing as it moved down the staircase. We anxiously followed behind.

"This world has been full of secrets for too long."

We continued to descend into a cold, metal room. In the room were three wires hanging from the ceiling and, sitting right in front of them, was a button in the shape of an eye.

"Where are we?" Phoenix asked.

"This is the Main Focus Gate. The door to the Atheiria... Plug your Focuses into those wires."

We did as instructed. I took the wire and plugged it into my Focus. My head jerked back and pulses of pain shot down from my brain to the rest of my body. The world around me went black. My senses faded. I couldn't feel the ground any more. I couldn't hear, taste, smell, or feel anything. I was floating in an infinite void.

But soon the void started to build a world around me. The void was filled with white. There was no ground but I could feel there was.

I could hear a soft breeze running past my ears. I could feel a reality that didn't exist. In front of me was the Silhouette. It moved.

The Silhouette walked closer to me on the floor that didn't exist. I felt an urge to walk towards it as well. Each step echoed. Resonated. It grew louder as we drew closer to each other. They went from footsteps, to jackhammers, to gunshots, to fireworks, to thunder claps. My ears felt as if they would explode, but I kept going. Soon, we stood face to face. It was the same height as me. Same build as me. It *was* me. Instinctively. Voluntarily. Unwillingly. I chose to. Take another step. I walked inside the Silhouette. It enveloped me, and took me to another layer of reality.

Within this layer, I found a man. He was old, his hair thinning and white. He wore round, wire frame glasses and all white clothes. He was sitting cross-legged on the non-existent floor.

"Who are you?" I asked him.

"You don't recognize the man who sits guarding his tower of failures? The man who saved Humanity from disorder after the Fall?"

"Wait... Locke?"

"I am Locke. The First Hegemon."

"But that doesn't make sense... You're dead!"

"My body is dead. My mind is alive."

"How?"

"Many years after I formed the Hegemony, I had Dr. Vallor build the Focus Network and the Atheiria. I would upload my mind to the network, live in the Atheiria, and keep watch on Humanity after my body dies. I would possess each Hegemon that came after me through the neural network formed by the Focus. Allowing my influence in the world to be eternal."

"Why? Don't you trust your own system?"

"I trust the system... not the ones following it. People say that if we remember history, we will never repeat our mistakes. Yet we always do. It is Human nature to create

problems for others. **We cause our own destruction. In order to prevent another Fall, I became a failsafe. In the rare chance anyone rises up and poses a threat, I just possess them and kill them and anyone else involved."**

"Then why create Damocles? He poses the biggest threat we've seen in a hundred and forty-two years."

"There are many factors at play. So first you must understand who Damocles is."

From the infinite white, Damocles walked forward.

Palming the front of his mask, Damocles removed it, revealing a man with long golden hair, a pointed chin and an emotionless stare.

It was Viceroy Micah!

"You faked his death?"

"Indeed."

"Why? Why create problems in the society you said was perfect?"

"Sometimes... people need a reminder. A reminder of past mistakes. By creating Damocles I could remind the masses of the danger and importance of war in a safe and controlled way... I controlled the people of Amestris, and faked the death of Micah to make him Damocles. I began to notice a distrust in the Hegemony—a sort of questioning, if you will. I needed a way to make them trust it again."

"How does making Damocles make people trust the Government more?"

"If all people are united against a common enemy, the person who defeats that enemy becomes loved, revered—however you wish to refer to it. I built the Hegemony by using Humanity's fear of the Fall. By reminding them of that fear, and then getting rid of it, it lowers the chances of another Fall happening to almost zero."

"So you killed the millions of people living in Xerxes to do it."

"It was for the greater good."

"Millions of innocent people are dead!"

"The ends will justify the means. The deaths of those

people were for the hope of utopia."

"Yeah, a utopia built on corpses."

"What do you do when there is an evil you cannot defeat by just means? By creating fear of mistakes, you keep people from making them. The entire Human world is run by fear. You do not break the law because you fear the consequences. You eat because you fear starvation. You love because you fear being alone. Those who break the law, those who do not love, just aren't fearful enough."

"..."

"I built this world on the mistakes of the old world. I built a tower on top of failures and I plan on adding another floor. History is the story of great men... and I am the greatest man. This is my story and I'm writing another chapter."

"You're writing it in blood."

"I already bear the weight of the world on my shoulders. What's a couple more pounds? You yourself are a product of the fear I amplified. One of the pawns I use to write my story."

"So why did you chose Ada, Phoenix and me?"

"Phoenix showed one of the best results in his Pod Group. Ada was just above him. You... You showed great strategic ability. But most important, you showed empathy. A good trait for a leader is to be able to relate with their subordinates. Do you remember Laura?"

"Yes."

"She's still waiting for you to return. Not Phoenix or Ada. Just you. Same thing with Judy. Even Elro."

"..."

"Hopefully you will."

"So I assume you want one of us to become Hegemon?"

"Indeed."

"Won't you just take control of us, like Bradley?"

"There will be no need. You see after this war is over, no

one will have the slightest thought of rebellion. I'll have intelligent leaders and, as a bonus, you're all young. Everyone will have even more trust in the Genetic Pairing system. True perfection is right around the corner."

"So how do you want this to end?"

"I want either you, Phoenix or Ada to launch an ultimatum against Damocles. Attack Amestris, take all the C.O.N.S.P.I.R.E. reactors and launch them into deep space to mark the end of an era. After that is done, one of you will be chosen as Hegemon, and I can't wait for the very tiny chance of a threat rising again."

"Then it'll all be over..."

"Correct."

Locke outstretched his hand for me to shake it. I was hesitant, but I shook his hand, shooting me back into the real world where Bradley's possessed body stared back at me, Phoenix and Ada.

"Welcome back," it said.

TURN 36.

Ragnarok Begins

"A crime is committed to end all crime. Evil destroyed with evil. Beautiful isn't it? Witnessing the glorious beginning of a new age of Humanity, built on the corpses of innocents. Xerxes was a sacrifice. A sacrifice that will bring about a new age that will never end, one that will never forget my story. A story written in blood. All for Utopia. All for peace. All for... Perfection."**
—CALL ENDED—

Bradley's possessed body looked at us, a slight smirk of pride on his face.

"I have sent word to Mendez. Troops will mobilize on Amestris in 30 minutes. Damocles has also been informed. He has now had plenty of time to set up defenses. I guess you could say this is... Ragnarok? Armageddon? Either way, the final war in Human history ends now."

A strange, twisted smile streaked across Bradley's face.

"If you win this battle, the Hegemony will face no more crime, no more trouble. No more innocents will be killed. Humanity will be cured. If you fail, I will activate C.O.N.S.P.I.R.E., destroying Amestris and all of Proxima B

with it. **The ultimate fear will be instilled in the minds of Humanity for all time. The end result for both is eternal peace. Humanity will continue to flourish under the fear of another Fall. A utopian society is inevitable, but which timeline will we see?"**

"We need to go," Phoenix said, his voice shaky. And he refused to look into the eyes of the Silhouette. He stepped closer to the staircase to get up to the Fleet Bay. Ada and I followed him up the stairs back to the Hegemon's room.

"How do you think this will end?" I asked.

"All I know, is that we can't let C.O.N.S.P.I.R.E. go off," Phoenix responded.

Ada panicked. "How will we even do that?" she said. "We'll have Damocles' soldiers to deal with. We don't know if any Swarm Machines will be there—we might as well just go with the second outcome!"

I attempted to reason with her. "We can't just sit there and let the entire planet get destroyed."

"The end result will be the same as if we stop it," Ada responded.

"But the entire planet will be gone!" Phoenix jumped back in.

"At least it's easier than trying to fight our way through hell!"

"Does that justify it for you?"

Ada hesitated. "I'm not saying I'm okay with it... Just, if all the C.O.N.S.P.I.R.E. reactors go off and Proxima B is destroyed, the fight will be over quickly. It'll all be over in a single, short burst."

"The black hole that forms from the reactions could just consume the planet, and if Xerxes says anything, all of that energy will be released instantly after. The Centauri System will be destroyed!" Phoenix explained. "Either we fight our way through hell, or we let an entire System be blown to bits. What do you choose?"

"... Fine. But I wish this could be easier," Ada gave in.

"Good, now we need to meet up with the others. This'll be a battle to remember." Phoenix led the way to the Fleet Bay.

The endless sea of students stood at attention with their Platoons in small yellow squares. Their Nano-Reactors glowed, looking like stars against the background of open space. After scanning the area, I ran over to my Platoon and took my place at the head of the square. On a magnificent platform, overlooking the gigantic army of students, stood Bradley. He had his mask on once again, which made it so the voice of the Silhouette could not be heard. It also hid his eyes, so no one would know he was possessed.

"Students," his voice was monotone as usual. "This Cycle, we make one last stand against Damocles."

A roar of determination exploded from the mouths of the students. Fists were raised to the heavens, and stomping feet made even the void of space shake.

The Silhouette extended its hand through Bradley, and a screen appeared in the Hegemon's palm. It was a full map of Amestris. "The enemy is in control of this territory."

Locke, as the Hegemon, pointed to the base of the Viceroy Tower making a red dot appear. "All C.O.N.S.P.I.R.E. reactors are housed here. That is our target. We will send all of you to Amestris to collect the C.O.N.S.P.I.R.E. reactors and launch them into space without them detonating. If even one of them detonates, all of the Centauri System will be destroyed. We have also detected five Swarm Machines guarding Amestris: Loki, Fenrir, Jormungand, Hrym, and Surtr."

The causes of Ragnarok...

"These machines will pose the greatest threat to Amestris and Proxima B. Destroy them first, then move to the tower. This fight will rely on your individual ability to think quickly, and develop your own plans. Failure or success, this will change the course of history. From the ashes will rise a new world, a world that has never been seen before. We will succeed; we will create a world that knows only peace!"

With a final, thunderous battle cry, every student ran for their ships, zipping out of the hangar at a speed faster than light, rushing out in white spheres, to a battle ground that would bring about a new era.

TURN 37.

He Who Would Eat the Sun

"This will be a battle that documents a split in the giant web that is time. Many possible timelines visibly forming. From this battle will rise my future. My world. A time that I strived to make. I will make a utopian world. After Ragnarok."

"Brandon?" Nina asked through the comms.

"Yeah?" Space was quiet. The stars were gently drifting past, and the blue light from the cockpit reflected slightly off the nano-glass.

"This really is the end..."

"Yeah."

"It all... escalated so fast." She sounded hopeful, yet also helpless.

"At least it will all be over soon."

The information the Silhouette gave me allowed me to have the tiniest bit of hope. *Every game has a way to win.*

"I hope you're right," she said. Then her voice grew shakier. "I don't want to die."

"Hey, you won't. You have your Nano-Reactor right?"

"It won't protect me if C.O.N.S.P.I.R.E. goes off... And it won't protect you."

She was right. Nothing could survive C.O.N.S.P.I.R.E. At least nothing that we were aware of. We really were fighting the shortest, but most important war in human history. Only four battles were fought, and this would make the fifth. Only the citizens of Xerxes had died, leaving the death toll at virtually zero in comparison to wars fought on Earth. Yet this war had become the most terrifying in written history.

"We'll win…" I attempted to reassure her.

The twin stars of the Centauri System came into view, and our targeting systems locked onto Proxima B. Our ships slowed to prepare for entry.

"Target in sight," Mendez cut in on the comms. "Keep formation until we enter Amestris."

Our ships dove down to the planet, becoming shimmering balls of flame upon contact with the atmosphere. Once stable, Amestris came into view. Holo-rails were active, and the Blaze Luminous was up. The tower was highlighted by the targeting system, making it illuminate a crimson red. Our ships held a steady course to the enemy Sector before one familiar symbol caught my eye. A purple eye flashed in front of a black figure. With sparks of red light flying off of it, the figure charged forward at blinding speeds.

"Get ready!" Mendez yelled.

It was a gigantic mechanical wolf. *Fenrir!* With fur made from strands of deep red light crystals. The wolf jumped upward, shattering the ground below it with a boom. With one massive mechanical paw, the machine slashed down an entire Platoon.

"Split and fire at the body!" Phoenix ordered.

I dove my ship downward and spun around, following after the wolf. Madyson brought down her Platoon and Lee's to fire at the machine's ribcage.

"Phoenix, scan it for a weak spot!" I yelled.

Fenrir opened its jaws, and a red light sparkled out. Its eyes sparked purple and a massive beam of plasma exploded from its jaws, ripping through our formation.

"Found it!" Phoenix blurted out.

"Where?" Ada asked.

"Right under its jaw, like in the myth," Phoenix responded.

"Perfect," Ada started. "My Platoon, join with Phoenix and draw its attention. Brandon, you go do what you usually do."

"I'm helping too!" Scarlet jumped in, her Platoon zipping above the wolf's head and shooting down at it. Quickly Phoenix and Ada followed, spiraling above Fenrir. Noticing this, the wolf's eyes glowed green. Its body sparked, producing a Blaze Luminous shield around it.

"Damn..." Madyson muttered.

Fenrir's eyes sparked purple again, and it fired another powerful blast at the ships overhead. When it did, the shield opened temporarily to let the blast through.

"That's our opening," I announced to my Platoon. We dropped lower to the surface and circled around the machine, waiting for another opening. Fenrir looked up at the spiraling ships once again, and the opening presented itself. I turned my engine up all the way, whipping around the shield, flying up and dropping down to the interior. Flipping the ship straight up, I fired all the shots I could possibly make at the massive wolf's jaw before looping back out the way I came.

Fenrir's shield shattered like glass, and the wolf looked up at the sky. With its dying breath, it fired one last beam into the heavens before being destroyed by a single, beautiful explosion. A resounding, joy-filled cheer went through the comms.

"Don't get too excited," Mendez cut in. "The battle's not over yet. We still need to reach Amestris. We have four more to go."

TURN 38.

A Swarm of Four

"**Fear is what governs the world. By bringing a fear of what will destroy peace, no one will act out of line. Humanity needs to be reminded of that fear. In order to bring about that fear... Keep playing.**"

Shards of Fenrir came crashing down after the explosion. It started to rain, blackening the sky, with sporadic sparks of lightning crashing within the storm. Mendez gave the order, and our ships continued on the path to Amestris.

"Only four more..." said Phoenix.

On the inside, I could hear my ship hum as we sped through the stormy air. Amestris was just some minutes away, but that only meant more trouble.

Soon enough we were in enemy territory. There were no people walking in the streets as we flew over the edge of the Sector. No street lights were on, and neither were the lights in any housing units. Only the tower was illuminated by the lights within it.

"We've gone pretty far without being attacked," Ada pointed out. The once bustling Sector was now silent and empty.

"Wait. Don't get comfortable," Phoenix responded.

We continued our course to the tower. The silence continued, leaving me restless. It was going too smoothly.

"Once we reach the tower, you each have Teleporters that will send the reactors into deep space. Once that's done, we'll hunt down Damocles and his soldiers." Mendez explained, before letting the silence seep back in. It was only the soft hum of the ship. We were finally in range to land until, "Hey what's th—"

An entire Division exploded mid-air. Shards of their ships crashing into the buildings below like tiny meteorites.

"Oh, shit!" Scarlet remarked. "There!"

Three purple eyes flashed, but I couldn't see the machines. My targeting system locked on to them and also detected another machine behind us. The three ahead drifted over to form a triangle, surrounding us.

"Hold formation…" Mendez ordered, sounding uncertain of how to handle the situation.

I scanned for a weak point in the machines, but I couldn't detect them. The red diamonds just hovered in place.

"Damn it, they're making us hold position," Ada started. "They're stalling for something."

"For what, though?" I asked.

There was a slight pause, before a terrifying realization. "They're trying to use C.O.N.S.P.I.R.E!"

"On what? Where would be the most important place to—The Sequence Academy!" I panicked. "Colonel, we need to move now!"

"No, they have us surrounded," Mendez responded.

"The Sequence Academy could be destroyed!" I attempted to reason with him.

"If we move, all of our ships will be destroyed, and the war will be over."

"Oh, to hell with it!" Phoenix's ship shot out of formation at one of the machines, with his Platoon following close behind.

"Dammit, Phoenix!" Mendez yelled. "All forces, divide and take on a machine. We have no choice now."

"There ya' go, Mendez!" Scarlet yelled out before breaking

formation and going after a machine.

The storm raged on as every Platoon broke off towards different machines. I charged my ship straight ahead at one of the red diamonds on my screen. I could hear shots, and small explosions going off behind me. The hum of my engine grew louder, until I and ten other Platoons came face to face with the Swarm Machine.

It hovered, holding a gigantic scepter like device that split in two at the head. A glowing ball of plasma was held between the prongs. On its back, three wide strands of light crystals danced in the wind of the storm. On its head was a pair of horns with a high arch. I scanned it. Loki had no weak point.

"Colonel Mendez..." I stammered. I didn't know what to do. "One of the machines has no weak point."

"What?" Mendez seemed just as confused as I was.

"Neither do the others," Madyson informed him.

"Keep fighting," Mendez ordered. "If things get too bad we can make them destroy the tower and we retreat."

"That will destroy the entire System!" Phoenix jumped in.

"It's a last resort."

Loki flew forward at our advancing ships. Its scepter glowed, and fired small shots at us, forcing us to split up. It zipped past, seeming to go to the center of the battle grounds. I flew after it, firing desperately at its back. It had no effect. My engine hummed louder and louder the faster I went. I was shooting like a mad man. Every single ship in the other ten Platoons that were with me fired endlessly, also to no effect.

"Loki's moving to the center," I warned everyone else.

"Why? What did you do?" Ada sounded like she was panicking, her voice growing more and more frustrated as the battle continued.

"I don't know!" I said. I wasn't doing any better.

Loki stopped, balling in on itself, emitting a beautiful emerald light, ripping apart nearby buildings, and absorbing them, making it glow even brighter.

"What the hell did you do?" Ada screamed.

Loki threw its arms out in a T pose, sending out a powerful pulse of green light. My engine cut out, along with those of the entire army. My ship started to drop out of the sky, throwing me around violently within. I frantically looked for any buttons to press, but there were none, just the smooth white walls around me. I tapped my Focus but there was no response. My Nano-Reactor had also shut off, and my heart sunk. I looked around for anything, literally anything.

"The glass!"

I balled up my fist, and began punching the glass with all the strength I could muster. Pounding, and pounding, and pounding. I felt one of my knuckles explode. Blood dripped down on the screen. I kept going, until the glass finally cracked. I flipped around and started kicking.

"One. Two. Three."

It shattered.

I fell through, grabbing onto the opening. Shards of glass pierced into my hands as I hoisted myself on top of the free-falling ship. Holding on for dear life, I looked out at the thousands of other ships plummeting down to the surface. The rain felt like rocks falling from the sky. My heart was pounding out of my chest, and I couldn't get any air. Through the wind I heard my Nano-Reactor buzz back to life. I also felt my Focus activate again. The engine of my ship however, for some reason, didn't reactivate. So I had no choice.

I looked around for any nearby buildings. I spotted the roof of a housing unit. I steadied myself on the spheroid ship, dropped my knees slightly, before pushing off and jumping for the roof. I flew forward, my arms flailing wildly in the stormy air. I slapped against the building, just barely grabbing the ledge. The shards of glass dug deeper into my flesh, sending a tingly, fractal like pain through my hand.

I managed to pull myself onto the roof, and looked out at the city. My ship's engine turned back on, shooting it straight down into the ground, crashing with a fiery boom. The blood from my hand was a glowing white cloud of nanites, and my knuckle was slowly re-constructing itself. Fires had started where the other ships crashed, smoke billowing up from multiple craters and destroyed buildings.

I scanned for Nina. She was three blocks down. I ran down the fire escape stairs, almost slipping. Once down I ran as fast I could. The orange blazes were battling against the endless rain.

And in the black sky, amongst the cracks of lightning that split the sky, stood the other two machines. Below them, approaching over the horizon, was another Swarm Machine.

I kept running towards Nina. My breath stinging in my lungs. When I saw her, she was running with six other Platoons to the Capsule Gate. The surviving members of the army were converging at this one place.

"Nina!" I yelled, running even faster. She turned around, with an expression of relief and pure joy.

"Brandon!" She ran at me too, hugging me as we met. "We need to go," she said. "Everything's going to shit here..."

"I know. I need to find Mendez."

"That's where we're all running. Gio, Emery, Dayami and Eric are already there. So is Mendez."

"Perfect."

We continued running. The rain somehow getting even harder. My uniform was soaked, but I kept going.

We soon arrived at the burning Capsule Gate, to a sea of students. Friends huddled together for warmth, some discussing what to do next, others panicking in search of someone they knew. Ryan ran up to me, horrified.

"Brandon, please... have you seen Quinn..?" he asked his voice shaky, and choked. "I can't find her... My Focus isn't detecting her... I was watching her ship from mine, and when our Nano-Reactors cut out and I saw it hit... a building."

"Ryan."

"Our Nano-Reactors weren't on..." He collapsed into painful sobbing, folding in on himself.

"I'm sorry."

"She can't be dead... We didn't even get to have our first Sequence game..."

"Ryan, she's gone."

I didn't know how to console him. Ryan was always a happy-go-lucky person when we were roommates, the type to enjoy everything and just live a free life. But now, he was in a corner he didn't know how to get out of.

"I'm going to go talk to Mendez. Everything will be alright."

I walked through the apocalyptic scene towards Colonel Mendez. On the way, illuminated by the fires of crashed ships, were others mourning the deaths of their loved ones and teammates.

"Colonel Mendez!" I called over to him.

"Yes..." he answered.

"I know what we can do," I answered.

"We can't do anything else..."

"Ada, Phoenix, and I will take our Platoons to the tower to get rid of C.O.N.S.P.I.R.E. while you take the surviving Units to keep the other Swarm Machines back. We can sneak in and teleport the reactors into deep space."

"What other choice do we have? This war has gone a direction I never thought possible," Mendez sulked. He had given up all hope, except this one last attempt. It was all we had. "I'll rally everyone, while you go. This is the ultimatum."

The storm raged on, smoke rising up to the darkness. Lightning sprinting across the sky. Loki looked down at us, with the other machines at his sides and below. The trickster was waiting.

TURN 39.

Ultimatum

"I will keep watching."

The storm raged on. The wind was freezing cold, and the rain felt like ice beating down on my soaked uniform. The flames set by the crashed ships were strewn about the ravaged Sector, inhabited only by students. I walked over to Phoenix and Ada, my Platoon following close behind. Phoenix stared up at the hovering machines. A desperate, helpless expression on his face.

"One more is on the way," he said, and glanced over at me. "We shouldn't have even done this. The end result would have been the same..."

"What would we have done then?" I asked. "It's better to go down swinging, right? I would've expected you to be the one to tell me that."

"Why are you here?" Ada bluntly asked. She was cold and stoic as usual, but seemed still unsure of what was going to happen.

"We're getting rid of C.O.N.S.P.I.R.E." I said.

"Those things are probably just gonna blow up the tower if we try. We'll die with Amestris," Phoenix explained.

"We won't die. The Silhouette needs us," Ada corrected him. "Either way, it'll still be bad."

"We'll have everyone else keep the machines occupied while we rush in and get rid of the reactors," I answered.

"What do we have to lose?" said Phoenix.

"I guess you're right..." Ada agreed.

Just then there was a thunderous boom that rolled up and back down the burning streets.

"Get your Platoons ready, the last Swarm Machine is almost here." I walked off and took my place behind Colonel Mendez, facing the tower.

The last Swarm Machine, Jormungand, was able to be seen in its entirety now. A mechanical serpent that made Loki look like a pet dog. Its head was slender, and had luminescent spikes poking off, like a crown.

Mendez stepped closer to the massive army. Ada and Phoenix stood next to me, our Platoons side by side.

Loki, Hrym, and Surtur descended from above, in front of Jormungand.

"Students!" Mendez's energy had returned. "Things have taken a turn for the worse. The battle to protect society as we know it has seemed to fail. But we have one last shot."

He pointed over at me, Phoenix, and Ada.

"They're the bullet. We're firing this shot and it better not miss. Your job is to keep those things from disturbing their mission. Keep them back at whatever cost. This war: It ends today!"

The students rose to their feet, to face the last threat. One last hurdle to jump. Some were ready to fight to avenge their fallen comrades. Some were fighting for the Hegemony. Some were fighting to prove themselves. Some didn't know what they were fighting for, but they felt the need to. All these reasons were the driving force, the spark that was needed.

I drew my Stun Gun, along with Ada and Phoenix. Our Units drew their weapons, along with the rest of the army.

With Loki taking the first step, and a powerful roar from Jormungand, we charged to our destinations. The booming stomps of the Swarm Machines, kept me running. I couldn't see what was happening behind me. All I saw was the tower. Screams resonated through Amestris, the sound of a plasma cannon firing in the distance. We were drawing closer.

Panting. The rain stung as I ran. My uniform was soaked, and cold; the wind didn't make it better. We were getting closer to the tower, getting closer to Damocles, getting closer to C.O.N.S.P.I.R.E. We had to win.

Ada broke off, slapped her hand against a license detector to open the massive steel doors. "Go! Go! Go!" she yelled.

We rushed in, letting the door slam shut behind us.

"Well…. We're in," Phoenix said in the comms.

"Great," Mendez answered, explosions going off around him. "Follow your map, then get out as fast as you can."

"Got it," Phoenix replied. "I feel bad leaving them out there to deal with those things."

The tower was quiet. There was a red carpet leading over to an empty reception desk, and random shrubbery covering the bits of the unnatural, white walls. I tapped my Focus to pull up the map of the tower.

"They won't be able to fight them off forever. This way," I called Ada over to the side of the door while I covered the other side.

Stun Gun in hand, I had two Snipers ready their bows for when we opened the door. I tapped the scanner, but no one was on the other side of the door. It was an empty, high ceiling hallway.

"What?" Ada asked. "No one's—what?" She stepped through the doorway. "This doesn't make sense… at least some guards should be here."

"This is probably some kind of trap," Phoenix pointed out. "We need to keep moving."

We took our Platoons through, weapons still drawn, watching everything. Our footsteps echoed through the hallway, bouncing through my mind. It was maddening, knowing I was walking in a room that could explode at any moment. Each echo was more tense than the last. I could hear my own breath; my heart was beating in my head, growing faster and faster.

We made it to a flight of stairs, and yet no one was guarding. Our path so far, had been un-interrupted. My palms grew sweaty as I held onto my Stun Gun. Once we made it down the stairs, my Focus illuminated the door a deep crimson red.

"This is it..." I whispered.

Tapping the sensor, I opened the door, revealing a large open room. The floor and walls were a clean white, housing hundreds of reactors. They were medium sized cubes, with two shimmering blue rings around them. They didn't look like much, but inside each was a mini particle accelerator. Powerful enough, if allowed, to destroy solar systems.

No one was protecting the reactors. The room was silent and motionless.

"This was too easy..." said Phoenix.

"We can... start sending away the reactors now, I guess," I said.

I walked into the room cautiously. After a couple seconds everyone else followed. We each walked over to the reactors, highlighted them, then tapped our Focuses. The reactors sparkled then, in a bright flash, disappeared, sent away to a far region of space.

All but one.

Nina stood in front of the last reactor, staring at it. Her arms were limp and I couldn't see her face. Her hair was messy as usual, but her stance was different.

"Nina?" I asked.

"You like this one don't you?"

"Wh—Why? Why are you here? Why are you in Nina?" I stammered.

The students who were with us jerked their heads back violently and their Focuses exploded. Their Nano-Reactors deactivated leaving one hundred forty-nine students lying pale and bleeding to death on the floor with holes in their heads where their Focuses should be.

"We won't be needing them."

Ada stepped back in horror. "You... You killed them..." Her voice and body were trembling.

Phoenix was pale. The fire that fueled him was blown out.

"I wanted you all to witness this. After all, you've won the game."

I was too scared to say anything. My knees were about to give out. I couldn't breathe.

"You've stopped the destruction of Proxima B; you've eliminated C.O.N.S.P.I.R.E.; you've defeated Damocles... The war is now over. Congratulations."

"Why.... why did you need to kill them..?" Phoenix was tearing up.

"The world needs a fear to govern them, and you all are part of this world."

"But you... killed them all. They didn't need this!"

"That was to make sure you don't try to stop me."

Nina smiled, her eyes pitch black.

"What are you doing?"

"I'm going to set off C.O.N.S.P.I.R.E."

"WHY?! You said we won right? Proxima B shouldn't be destroyed!" I attempted to reason with it.

"I said nothing about Amestris."

"Why are you using Nina to do it?" I needed to find a reason. I needed Nina. She couldn't die. I didn't want her to.

"In this game, you got the most points. This last attack on Amestris is under your name. Since that's the case, the war was won by you. You're the next Hegemon."

"Wh... what?" Giovanni's blood reached my boot.

"I know you like Nina the most. Using her will make you fear me even more. That way, you won't make a decision outside of my will. The civilians of the world will fear another event like this and fear another Fall... And you will fear me doing to you, what I did to them. Congratulations Brandon Simons... You've completed my game. You will now become Hegemon. Just as I am the Savior of the Fall, you are the Ender of War."

Eric, and Dayami lay lifeless at Nina's feet, pale, with blood pouring out the sides of their heads. My entire Platoon was dead. Soon Nina would be too. Their blood was on *my* hands.

"I did this...?"

Phoenix had turned away, his face buried in his hands. Ada was balled up, gripping her own hair.

"I... no..."

Nina picked up the last reactor.

"Any of you try to teleport this, I will kill you."

She twisted it and pulled upwards, revealing a keypad. The Silhouette, through Nina, punched in *F-E-A-R*, and set the timer for five minutes.

"Now... You should probably leave. Unless you want to die too."

"I'm not dying," Phoenix croaked. "I'm the Immortal. My Platoon would want me to live..."

Ada stood up, eyes unblinking. Walking out of the room, still gripping her hair, she had been broken into submission.

"Come on Brandon..." Phoenix said, grabbing my arm, pulling me away from the room. He messaged Mendez that C.O.N.S.P.I.R.E. was accidentally activated and we needed to evacuate the Sector.

I caused this.

I was leaving Nina. She was going to die with the sector she was born with.

Once out of the tower, the rain had stopped. Loki, Hrym, Surtur, and Jormungand were still ravaging the sector. Fires had spread, ashes of destroyed buildings floating up into the sky. The sun was setting, leaving the sky a light orange red. Mendez was ordering the students to run for the Spire to teleport out. Phoenix was still dragging me by the arm, I couldn't hear what was going on around me. All I heard was the explosions of my Platoon's Focuses, over and over again. We reached the Spire, and Phoenix threw me into the spinning blue diamond, into the barracks.

A total of six hundred twenty-seven students died in Ragnarok.

TURN 40.

Donning the Mask

"The game is finished. The victor is decided. Above him sits a watcher, fear hovering above his head. The pawn that was promoted, and governed by the Sword of Damocles. A new game starts as the old has finished. It is truly a beautiful process. A process that I rule. A system that is perfect. A species that is now. Me."

3/27/142 P.C.W.

I looked around the large, dark room searching for a window. Anything that would let me look at Amestris. The room was lit by the soft blue glow of the Teleport Point, slightly reflecting off of a small rectangle-like spot in the edge of the room. I pushed my way through the huddling masses of students. I needed to see. I needed to see. I needed to see.

I crouched down at the small window, looking down at the planet. The surface was green, with little ponds set randomly about the Amestrian Sector. The Sector itself was a pleasant grid of triangles, illuminated by the streets set ablaze.

There was a small, dancing twinkle. The slightest sparkle. Then dark. An infinitely black point that covered only the tiniest bit of Amestris. The fires went out, the triangles disappeared, the green became brown, and any hint of life withered away before...

Boom.

A crackling, white flash of pure energy released in an instant, expanding like a cloud, incinerating everything it touched. When the light was gone, Amestris was gone. Nina was too.

"Hey..." Ryan said as he walked up to me.

I didn't respond, or look up at him.

"You don't need to respond" Ryan said. "I don't know where to go... I want to resign. You might as well too. Quinn is dead... The war is over. I just—I don't know. We only served like, four months? And we did six times the work of every other Generation that's been here... We can quit now. Come with me. It'll be like when we were roommates, right?"

"No, I can't," I answered. "I can't quit."

"Why not? What do you mean?"

"I'm the next Hegemon..." I responded.

"What? You don't know that."

"I am."

I still didn't look at him. Only at what used to be Amestris.

"The war just ended!" Ryan said. "They couldn't have decided that early. Where's Nina?"

"Down there," I said, and poked the window.

"Oh... Wait, she stayed behind?" His voice was getting confused, his speech failing to function. "So she- she did—*she* activated the reactor?"

"I told her to."

No.

"Why?"

"To end the war."

"You could have just gotten rid of all the reactors and we could have just ran!"

I didn't respond.

"You're not actually going to be Hegemon, are you?"

I nodded.

3/28/142 P.C.W.

The students were all gathered in the stadium quietly awaiting the words of Bradley. Sitting in a small pocket on the field, were the news stations of every sector of the Hegemony, fidgeting, with patience that was quickly dropping.

Bradley warped onto the stage. Behind his translucent podium and I sat in between Ada and Phoenix, watching the man behind the mask, not seeing Bradley behind it, but the Silhouette.

We knew what was about to happen.

"Greetings, Hegemony," Bradley spoke. The mask hid the possessed, black eyes. "In the words of the first Hegemon, Locke Jonah, 'War is a disease that has plagued humanity, yet it is necessary for us to progress and build on our mistakes.' The war against Damocles was, hopefully, the last war humanity will ever face. A war that showed to us the dangers of forgetting what the past has taught us. We activated C.O.N.S.P.I.R.E. in Amestris to destroy Damocles' base of operations, forcing him and his minions either to die or to flee to the surrounding Sectors that have been put on high alert."

He used us all...

"Before doing so, we sent all C.O.N.S.P.I.R.E. reactors into an empty region of the galaxy so that this terrible threat would be eliminated. Amestris and Xerxes are the new battle scars of humanity, constant reminders of this war. The millions that perished will be remembered, and their deaths will be the fuel for a new era of humanity. A new era that will be marked by a new leader."

There was a slight mutter from the large crowd.

"The student who organized and sparked the fire that drove us to this final battle. Brandon Simons."

My Military ID appeared on the screen behind Bradley.

I hated him. I hated the Silhouette. I hated the fate I had to accept.

"This is the student who will lead humanity in a brighter age. The age that came after thousands of years of turmoil and struggle. This war was not its own. It was the continuation of the Conspiracy War. The war that was for the control of planet Earth that ended with the planet's demise. The war that is now over, that was spawned through greed, bigotry, and the imbalance in the rights of humans. All of which were fueled by fear. With this war over, peace shall ensue. We shall all be one species that is not segregated by meaningless traits. This peace shall never be broken. It will last for as long as humanity exists. A humanity led by Brandon Simons."

How will this new world work?

3/29/142 P.C.W.

I stood before the throne of Bradley, on the crimson carpet that led to him. Around me were strangers, standing around me, proud and ecstatic about the new era that was just beginning. None of them were my friends. I couldn't escape the memory, phantom images wherever I looked. Holes in their heads where their Focuses should be, blood pouring from them. All except Ada and Phoenix. The strangers cheered, clapped, and whistled as I walked towards Mendez. All except Ada and Phoenix. Mendez had a hole in his head where his Focus should be. On the ground I saw my Platoon, all dead on the ground, a memory I couldn't escape. I kept walking, their blood tracking behind me. Lights flashed, I could see C.O.N.S.P.I.R.E. going off in the distance. The constant sound of my Platoon falling to the floor in my head. I kept walking. Bradley, still in his mask, sat proudly on his throne, watching me accept my fate. Mendez held the black jaw frame of my mask before me. The cheering grew louder as I reached for the mask. Ada and Phoenix, knew what it all took. It was all fake. I grabbed hold of the mask. Locke killed my Platoon, the citizens of Xerxes, any of Damocles' soldiers that were found, and Nina. All for making a *"utopia."* I didn't want this. I lifted the mask frame onto my head, clicking the button. The chrome mask materialized around my head, the visor concealing my eyes, but I could still see the world. I was Hegemon. I was grabbed by the arm and flung into a story I didn't want. I hated it. I hate it. I will hate it. The roar from the crowd resonated once more through the massive room. I didn't know what I was fighting for the entire war. I could have resigned after two months, but I didn't. And now, I would lead humanity into a beautiful future that was built on the needless slaughter of thousands. I hated it. I hate it. I will hate it. I had no choice. I either play the part now, or die. Nina was my example.

5/3/001 Post Damocles.

I sat on the throne. The seat was padded crimson velvet. The arm rests were cold, rigid iron. I sat there waiting, sitting in the blood of the Earth.

Ada walked in, a Colonel now. She had taken Mendez's role. She came in with the usual, cold and emotionless glare. "Hey."

"Hey."

"Nearly sixty percent of the Amestrians who aided Damocles have been arrested. The executions begin in five Cycles."

"And Damocles himself?"

"Still evading capture."

"Where's Phoenix?"

"He resigned a couple Cycles ago… He was quite torn up."

"I understand it."

She hesitated. "What about you?"

"I hate it here."

"I get it. I wanted to resign too, but this is all I've known. I couldn't just leave. You don't get the luxury of leaving. You essentially have a gun pointed to your head by the Silhouette."

"Please go."

"Yes, sir." She hesitantly turned to the door, carefully walking out. "I'm sorry."

Humanity had been cured from war. Anyone that even seemed to be acting out of line was either possessed and had their memories altered, or went missing and erased from everyone else's memory. I didn't lead. The Silhouette did. I was a figurehead, just like Bradley. Only this time, I wasn't possessed. I was forced to watch how humanity flourished because of the deaths of so many people. There were no problems. I hated it.

TURN 41.

Masks

DATE NOT FOUND
Behind the mask was me, recently a 16-year-old boy. A boy that was part of a great deception. The boy that won the game, and paid for the win with the lives of his friends. I did so, not knowing it would cost as much as it did. Deep down I knew that this game was "for the greater good," but this "greater good" was obtained through means that I hated. But to that I say did the ends justify the means? Is a life of eternal peace and happiness really worth the lives of those that were close to you? The Hegemony became a world run by a hidden, subconscious fear of breaking the peace that was so long sought after. Fear of opposing the Government that beat C.O.N.S.P.I.R.E. But from that fear came a utopia. A utopian dystopia. A world that, on the surface, seems pure and calm. But if you look carefully, you can see the smudges: the children born with birth defects who were killed, simply because they did not fit the mold; the Immortals who are being tortured and experimented on. These things I can't change. I have a gun to my head, held by a man who doesn't exist. The world has no more problems, only advancement. Society has become a machine built on one universal fear. Those who are not affected by this fear are quickly erased.

————— ◆ —————

"Hello Brandon."
The voice resonated within my mind.
"Yes?"
"You have been serving for quite some time now. My goal has been accomplished…"
"Am I free?"
I wanted to be free. But if I were what would I do with myself? I know nothing else now.
"No."
"…"
"I have something to show you. Something to bring this all to a proper close."
"It's all to your benefit, no one else's. I don't want to see it."
"My desires, ambitions and resolve have led you to the very top. I have also led Humanity to a point that will never wither."
"Why did you need to wrap us all into this..?"
"Would you have preferred if someone else suffered the same way you do?"
"…"
"Go down to the Focus Gate, then go to the level below it."
I didn't want to. But still, I stood up from my throne, motioning for the entrance to rise. The gears scraped against one another, groaning as the gate rose, allowing me to descend into the dark room housing the Focus Gate, the room in which I met Locke, the room that helped reveal that my fate was orchestrated by one man. Behind the neural connectors was a small, wooden door. The sign above the door, displayed an eye. Just one. Not glowing. Just a regular eye.
"I thought we were done with secrets… I thought this was all over."

"It's not. It will be when you go through that door."

"What is it?"

"Open it."

I grabbed the knob. It was cold, somewhat rusted. I opened the door, and on the other side, read *Immortal Room*. The room was damp, empty and dark. Only the faint purple glow lighting the way. I followed the hall down to a small glass containment room.

Inside the large white room sat a girl with her arms chained to the wall.

It was unmistakable. She was short, with green eyes. And a head of messy, ginger hair.

———◆———

CPSIA information can be obtained
at www.ICGtesting.com
Printed in the USA
BVHW031918121219
566499BV00001B/49/P